LOVE, SEX AND THE SINGLE MOM

PART 3

BY: SULTANA SAMS

ACKNOWLEDGEMENTS

I am very excited to have completed part 3 of Love, Sex and the Single Mom. This is my very first series and I can't wait to complete more. To everyone who supported me and encouraged me to write part 3, thank you very much. It is you all's excitement about my books that kept me excited to continue on writing.

To my kids Tey'on, Tamia, and Tania, I love you! You are the best support system ever! Thanks for helping me out at book fairs and understanding that I need my writing time. You three are my inspiration and motivation!

CHAPTER 1

NITRA

I moaned as Monty licked my pussy. The way he licked it made it seem like he was a hungry, starving man. He licked my clit while he slowly stuck his finger in and out of my vagina. Slowly he would lick then he would speed up. That shit was driving me crazy. As he continued, I screamed as I came in his mouth. Still hearing his slobbering sounds, it was obvious that he was licking every drop of my cum.

After I caught my breath, we kissed. He lay on his back and I began to kiss on his neck. Slowly, I worked my way down his chiseled body. I kissed his neck, then his chest and sucked his nipples. His dick got rock hard when I did that. Seeing his hard dick made my mouth water. Immediately, I took his dick inside of my mouth. Slowly, I sucked until his entire dick was in my mouth.

"Damn baby!" Monty was saying. "This is why I'm in love with your ass!"

I continued sucking and spitting on his dick. Abruptly, he snatched his dick out of my mouth. "Baby, where the hell is that smoke coming from?" he yelled, jumping out of the bed. Looking around, I noticed clouds of thick smoke creeping into the room.

"What the hell!" I screamed. I quickly put on the nightgown that I'd taken off earlier. Monty had put his jeans on. "There must be a fire somewhere!"

Monty grabbed my hand and said, "Let's try to get out of your room window. There's no telling what part of the house it's coming from. We got to get out of here now!" I was in panic mode. We ran to my room window. Monty tried opening it but it seemed stuck.

"I think it's locked!" I said. Reaching for the latch, I unlocked the window. My eyes had started to water and burn. I tried to open it using all my strength. Monty moved me to the side and tried to open it also but it wouldn't budge.

"Why won't this damn window open?" Monty asked. He kept trying to get it open.

"Damn, I forgot that Kevin had it nailed shut! He didn't want to worry about break-ins because he was always working!" I yelled out.

"His ass didn't worry about fires! We have to either break the window or try to make a run for the front or back door!" Monty said. Looking around the room, I knew that he was looking for something to break the window with. Coughing as the smoke filled the room even more; I spotted my cell phone and grabbed it.

"That won't break the window!" Monty yelled. When he began to cough, I got really nervous. The smoke was starting to affect him.

"I just want to call the police and have them on the way!" I yelled at him.

"Ok, I'm going to have to break the window with my hand," he told me.

Dialing 911, I was happy when the operator answered. "I think my house is on fire! Smoke is everywhere! My address is 845 Kettle Drive! Please come now!"

"Ok ma'am," the operator said. "Where are you in the house.

"I'm in my bedroom! Please just come to 845 Kettle Drive now!" I yelled. Just as I said this, I heard the sound of glass breaking. After wrapping his arm with his shirt, Monty had used his arm to break the glass.

"Ma'am, we're on the way. Please try to stay calm," the operator was saying into the phone. Ignoring her, I ran over to the window. I helped Monty as he pulled the remaining pieces of glass out of the window.

"Climb out first," he told me.

With my leg shaking, I started to put my leg out of the window first. I could barely see it was so dark. My room window would put us in the backyard. Deciding to check my surroundings, I pulled my leg back and put my head through the window. Heavy smoke was coming from the side of the house.

"Baby hurry!" Monty told me coughing.

Nervous, I put my right leg out of the window and ducked my head so that it wouldn't hit the top of the window pane. After some uncomfortable bending, I had my leg and my head out of the window. Slowly, I pulled the rest of my body out of the window and took the small jump down to the ground. I ran as far back away from the house as I could. Monty came out behind me. We coughed and looked around. The house was burning from both sides now. The fire was slowly spreading to the back. What the hell was going on? I thought to myself. The smoke was beginning to get heavier and our eyes were burning. Monty and I held each other and coughed. It was a sound of relief when we heard the fire trucks and police sirens.

CHAPTER 2

TASHA

What the fuck is happening? I thought as Mom continued to try to get free from Ty to fight Aunt Kathy.

"It wasn't what you think," Bernard was trying to explain as he zipped his pants. It was disgusting! His old ass!

Furious, I said "Why the fuck would you marry my damn Mom and do some shit like this?" Looking over at Aunt Kathy, I said, "And what kind of sister are you? Get the fuck out of my house!"

Lacy looked speechless. Aunt Kathy headed towards the door and said, "I'll get out! Come on Lacy! No one said anything when that drunken bitch fucked my man years ago!"

Mom, who was still being held by Ty, said "Bitch that was high school! You're just an old jealous hoe. You ain't shit and your hoe ass daughter ain't shit either!" She broke loose from Ty and started punching Aunt Kathy again. Aunt Kathy tried to fight back but Mom was too fast for her. Somehow, I managed getting between them again. Ty grabbed Mom again, this time he escorted her up the steps.

Aunt Kathy acted like she wanted to go after Mom and I grabbed her. "You need to get the fuck out of my house," I told her sternly. For her to do this and at her sister's wedding celebration was gross!

"I'll leave," she told me, snatching away from me. "Fuck her. She ain't shit. Just like your ass ain't shit. Your ass lucky that baby was Ty's. Hoe!"

"You're lucky you're my aunt!" I yelled at Aunt Kathy. "You've always been a jealous, old bitch! Now get the fuck out of my house before I forget you're my aunt and beat your old ass!"

Sandy grabbed my arm. She wanted to make sure that I didn't hit Aunt Kathy.

"Now hold up," Lacy had the nerve to say. "Don't talk to my mom like that. I know you're upset but still don't disrespect her."

This bitch had nerve! "Bitch, you and your mom get the fuck out!" Sandy grabbed me as I headed towards Lacy. I started pushing Lacy towards the door. Lacy jerked away from me but she went to the door and her and her mom left. The bitch had the nerve to slam the door behind them!

Turning to look at Sandy, I was bewildered. "What the fuck just happened?" I asked her. Out of the corner of my eye, it dawned on me that Bernard was still here.

"Leave!" I told him. My phone started ringing as he started explaining.

"It wasn't my fault. She pulled my pants down so fast," he mumbled to me. He must have thought I was born yesterday. Reaching the phone, I noticed the caller had hung up.

"Get the fuck out!" I screamed at him. Nervously, he walked towards the door.

"I promise it wasn't my fault," he said, grabbing the knob on the front door.

"Leave now!" I told his ass for the last time. My phone started ringing again. Glancing at the phone, I noticed the call was Anonymous.

"Hello," I answered as I gave Bernard a nasty look. He got the picture and finally went out of the door. Sandy went to lock it behind him.

"Sis," Nitra said on the other end of the call.

"Hey! Where's your ass at?" I asked her. "So much has happened! Get over here! Mom needs you!"

Nitra coughed as she said, "Sis my house caught fire. The ambulance is taking me to the hospital for smoke inhalation. They let me call you right quick. Meet me at Cedars Hospital now!" She was still coughing as she said, "I got to hang up!"

Standing there with my mouth open, I didn't say a word as she hung up.

"What's wrong?" Sandy asked.

"Nitra said her house caught fire and she's being taken to Cedars Hospital for smoke inhalation," I told her.

"Oh no!" Sandy said. "We got to go make sure she's ok!"

"Ty!" I yelled up the steps as I scrambled to find my keys and purse. He came running down. Mom was behind him.

"We got to go to the hospital! Nitra's house caught fire!" I told him. Panic started to set in. I was pacing back and forth.

He came rushing down the steps and hugged me. "Calm down baby," he said. "Let's go. I'll drive and you can explain everything in the car."

Ty, Sandy, Mom and I scrambled out the door and jumped in his car. I tried to calm down. Tonight had gone from good to bad to worse!

CHAPTER 3

NITRA

The ambulance ride seemed quick. Within minutes, we were pulling up to the back of the Emergency Room and I was being lifted out of the stretcher. I'd been coughing uncontrollably that's why they insisted on taking me to the hospital. Smoke inhalation was serious, so I didn't fuss. There was an oxygen mask on my nose and it did make me breathe much better. The smoke from the flames were strong and even being outside near the smoke affected our breathing.

Monty had ridden in a separate ambulance. He had cuts from breaking the window and the smoke seemed to affect him a lot more than me. He'd been wheezing before the ambulance arrived. "How the hell did the house catch fire?" I thought to myself as I was wheeled into a small room.

Minutes later, nurses were giving me water to sip and asking me questions about my health and medical insurance. They'd given me a breathing treatment and it was helping me breath much better. The water was nice and cold too. Shortly after the nurse took all of my information, the door opened and police officers walked in. The nurse exited as they entered.

"Hi Miss," one officer said to me "We need to ask you a few questions."

"Ok," I said.

"Do you know how your house caught fire?" he asked.

"No, I have no clue. Maybe there was a gas leak or something? I don't know. I didn't cook today, so I couldn't have left the stove on. Never in a million years did I think anything like this would ever happen," I told him. The reality of my house being on fire set in. Had everything been destroyed?

"Ma'am, there was evidence of arson found at the scene," the officer continued.

"Arson?" I asked. "You mean to tell me someone deliberately set my house on fire? To try to hurt me? What if my kids had been home?"

"You have kids?" he asked. "How many kids do you have and what are their names and ages? Who else lives in the house with you?"

He hammered me with questions and I answered each one while in shock. Happiness came over me when the door opened and Tasha, Mom, Ty and Sandy walked in. Tasha came and gave me a hug. Mom was behind her. She looked liked she'd been crying. I assumed she was worried about me. She hugged me tight after Tasha was done.

"What happened baby?" Mom asked. "We were wondering why you never showed up."

Before I could answer, the police cut in. "We just have a couple of more questions then we'll leave you to your family. Is there anyone that you could think of that would want to harm you?"

"Harm her?" Tasha asked. "Why would you ask that?"

"He says they found evidence of arson," I told her.

"Arson? Someone purposely set your house on fire? Who the hell would do that? What if my niece and nephew had been in there?" Tasha looked panicky as hell.

"Calm down," Ty told her. "So much went on tonight. You have to keep calm baby."

"So much went on?" I asked. "What else happened?"

"You don't want to know," Tasha said. She looked at Mom.

"Mom, I'm sorry to ruin your wedding celebration gathering. Where's Bernard?" I asked.

The distraught look on Mom's face told me that something horrible had happened. So, was Mom crying before she learned about my fire? What the hell was going on? And where the hell was Bernard?

CHAPTER 4

SANDY

Nitra had a confused look on her face. She didn't know about what happened earlier with her Aunt Kathy and Bernard. So much had happened, my head was spinning. Though we weren't related by blood, this was my family. Tasha and I were like sisters and I planned on being here for her and her family.

"Tasha, let's go to the cafeteria and get something to eat and drink while Nitra finishes up with the police. You need to relax a bit," I told her.

"Good idea," Ty said. "Come on. Let's all go down."

"I'm staying here with my baby," Tasha's mom said, referring to Nitra.

"Ok cool. We'll bring you both some food back up," I told her. It hurt to know what she had just gone through with her sister and her new husband.

A few minutes later, we were sitting in the cafeteria. We'd ordered and had placed a takeout order for Ms. Karen (Tasha's mom) and Nitra.

"What a day!" Tasha said. She was sipping on her iced tea. She'd gone through so many different emotions today that she was frazzled and shook up.

"Yes, it's been crazy! I'm so glad that Nitra is ok. Who would set her house on fire?" I questioned. Shit, I was on edge too!

"Probably Kevin's crazy ass," Tasha said. "He's so damn mad about what happened and he is suing her for custody of the kids."

"But the fire could have killed her. I don't think he would do that," I said. Kevin was acting crazy lately but I didn't think he was capable of setting his own house on fire.

"Well, who else?" asked Tasha. Ty sat next to her rubbing her arm and trying to calm her down. I just shook my head because I didn't have any answers for her. Maybe some kids in the neighborhood did it. It could have been a prank gone too far. The sound of my phone ringing took me out of my thoughts.

"Hello?" I answered.

"Sandy, I need you!" Lee yelled into the phone. He was breathing really hard as if he was out of breath.

"Look," I told him clutching my teeth. "Don't call me."

"Sandy please! This is life and death. Please pick me up on Cedar and Trillville Road. I jumped out of my car because I was being shot at. I'm ducked off. Please come get me now. I'll see your car." Lee hung up without giving me a chance to say anything else.

After staring at the phone for many seconds, I looked up to see Tasha and Ty looking at me.

"What's going on?" Tasha asked me. "Who was that?"

"It was Lee," I told her. "I got to go!" Without further explanation, I jumped up from the table and speed walked out of the hospital. I didn't know what I was getting myself into but Lee was Lea's father and I had to help him for her sake.

~

About twenty minutes later, I pulled up to the intersection of Cedar and Trillville Road. It was dark and felt spooky. He'd said that he would see me so he'd better hurry because I wasn't sticking around long. Seconds later, I saw a

19

figure walking toward my car. I got scared as hell. As the person got closer, I saw that it was Lee so I unlocked my doors.

As soon as he jumped in, I pulled off. "What the hell is going on?" I asked.

"I told you that I owe people. That's why I was desperate enough to break in your house. I got to get them that money!" Lee sounded panicky.

"How much?" I asked.

"$30,000 will squash everything. But don't think I'm trying to get you to pay it. I have a way to get it. It's a risk but I have no choice," Lee said. "I just need to duck off for a couple of days and plan everything. Then I'll make the call letting them know I got their money with interest."

My head was spinning as I shook it back and forth. "Look, I'll give you the damn money. Don't do anything stupid! Just pay it back!"

Lee shook his head. "No, I'm not going to take your money. That's to take care of our daughter. It's time that I man up."

"Lee, it wasn't long ago that you broke into my house for the money! Why wouldn't you accept me giving it to you? Lea needs her father. She misses you but of course I can't let her around you. You have too much going on! Take the damn money! I'll still be straight and have some left," I told him.

Lee thought about it for a minute. He shook his head. "Can you please just take me to a room out of town? I need time to think."

"Out of town where?" I asked him.

"Anywhere as long as it's about an hour from the city," he said.

Shaking my head, I headed to get on 95 South. It was a good thing Lea was with my mom. It was going to be a long night. How could so much happen in just one day? What the fuck was Lee getting me involved in?

CHAPTER 5

TASHA

When Sandy ran out of the hospital, I didn't know what to think. There was no energy in me to go after her. This day had been wild enough already and I needed to tend to my family. I would call Sandy later. I prayed everything was ok on her end. Ty and I gathered the food we'd ordered and headed back to Nitra's room.

Walking into her room, I was relieved that the police were gone. "What did they say?" I asked Nitra.

"They were just asking do I know of anyone who would set my house on fire on purpose and other questions. I'm exhausted and I need some clothes," she said looking at her hospital gown. She had to shower and change into the gown because her clothes were smoke filled. "They're going to observe me for a few hours and then I'll be going home later tonight."

"I'll get you some clothes," I told her. "I'll have to get you something from my house for now. Damn sis, I'm just realizing you lost everything in the fire. Do you think Kevin had something to do with this?"

"No," she shook her head. "We could have died in that fire. Kevin wouldn't kill the mother of his kids."

Shaking my head, I wasn't convinced. Then, I thought about what she said. "Did you say we? Who else was in the house?" I asked her.

Nitra looked at me but didn't say anything. That told it all. "Oh my God! It probably was Kevin if Monty was in the house! Where is Monty now?"

"He's in another room here. The police are speaking with him now. We've been texting but haven't seen each other since we got here," Nitra said.

"You're still messing with that man who ruined your marriage?" mama said looking shocked. Tears started flowing from her eyes. The events with Bernard and Aunt Kathy earlier were finally getting to her. She broke down and I went to hug her. Ty rubbed her back. He was such a great guy.

"I'm sorry mama," Nitra said. "We fell in love."

"Nitra, some things happened with mom and Bernard tonight. I'll tell you about it later but they broke up already. That's why she's sensitive," I said.

"Oh no! I'm so sorry mom! What happened?" she asked.

"I'll tell you about it later," I told her. "We're going to take mom home and then I'll bring you back some clothes."

"Ok," Nitra said. The look on her face was a mix of sadness and bewilderment. My poor sister's house had burned down. My poor Mom wasn't even back from eloping a week and her sister had betrayed her. What more could my family take?

CHAPTER 6

NITRA

Mom and Bernard were broken up? I thought as they left. They'd just eloped last week and their celebration was tonight! What the hell had happened so fast? It had been so long since I'd seen my mom cry. She was always tough. If I'd been to the event instead of fucking Monty, we wouldn't have been in the house when it caught fire. Maybe I could have prevented whatever had happened with her and Bernard? It had to be a minor disagreement. The marriage couldn't really be over already. Or could it?

So many thoughts were running through my head. I was in a daze staring in space and didn't even notice the room door open.

"Baby," Monty said. Startled, I turned in the direction of the voice and saw Monty walking in the door.

"Hey baby," I told him. He came over and hugged me.

"I'm so glad you're ok," he told me.

"Baby, I'm so glad we're both ok. We could have died in that fire!" Thinking about what happened had me frazzled again. He sat beside me on the hospital bed and gave me a hug. Noticing a bag in his hand I asked, "What's in the bag?"

"It's some clothes and underwear to put on. They're new. I called and told my brother everything that happened. Knowing you probably lost everything in the fire, I asked him to purchase you something to put on. He also brought me one of my outfits to put on. You know I've been staying with him ever since I broke up with Missy," Monty told me.

"That was so sweet of you to think of me," I told him. "Tasha is going to bring me something but I'm glad that I don't have to wait on her. I hate this hospital gown."

Looking in the bag, I pulled out some underwear. I tore off the price tag and slipped them on. There were some jeans and a T-shirt that I slipped on too. They'd thought of everything. His brother had purchased me some comfortable flats to slip on.

"Your brother thought of everything," I said. "Please tell him thank you from me."

"No problem. I'll tell him. But, you do know that I told him what to get right?" Monty said and laughed. For the first time that night, I smiled. There was something about this man that gave me butterflies no matter how rough things in my life seemed to go these past few months.

After I was fully dressed, I sat back down next to him. Looking into his eyes, I kissed him. Once we came up for breath I asked, "Baby what am I supposed to do? My house is destroyed. All of my belongings and kids' belongings are destroyed." While leaning against him, I started sobbing again. My life was really falling apart.

"All of that is replaceable baby," Monty said while rubbing my back. "I'm just glad you're ok. We're ok. And I thank God that your babies weren't home."

"I thank God too," I said sobbing.

A few minutes later, the nurse walked in. She informed me that they just needed us to take some inhaler test again and then we could be released soon. She left out to get the materials needed for the test. She'd preferred to give Monty his test in his own room but he refused to leave me. He knew that I was feeling emotional.

Monty sat on the sofa chair that was in the room for visitors. He said it was more comfortable than the bed. Smiling at his attempt to take my mind off of things, I sat on his lap and said, "I'm falling for you Monty. I don't know how this happened."

"I've already fell for you," he told me. "I love you girl. That's why I can't stay away from you."

"I love you too," I admitted to him. It was crazy but what started off as friendship turned into an affair. The affair turned into real love even though we each hurt people in the process.

"Baby, the police said the fire was intentionally set," I told him.

"I know," he said with a worried look on his face. He tried to keep a straight face but I knew that he was worried.

"Do you think someone wanted to hurt me? Or do you think maybe some teens in the neighborhood pulled some type of prank that went bad? They said they would let me know all the details once they gathered and analyzed everything."

"I don't know baby," he said shaking his head. "We just have to let the police do their investigation and see what they find out."

It was easy for me to tell that he had other thoughts in his head but didn't want to say anything. Addressing the elephant in the room I said "Do you think it was Kevin? Tasha immediately accused him."

"I can't say," said Monty. "He could be upset that I was in his house with you."

"It's our house," I corrected him. "And I tried to work things out with him but he didn't want to. Therefore, the house belongs to me and our kids. Monty, I don't think he would do something like this. We've been together since high school. He wouldn't want to kill me."

Monty just shook his head. "Well maybe he just wanted to scare you and it went too far. I don't know how the fire happened."

"What about Missy?" I asked him. "Ever consider that her bitter ass could have done it?"

Monty shook his head. "Hell no! She's not crazy enough to risk doing time and being away from our kids. Maybe she's crazy enough to fight you but not do this."

Still sitting in his lap, I looked into his face. Was he delusional? "Baby, she damn near held me captive in a room! What if I didn't fight them off? There is no telling what would have happened. She's as much as a suspect as Kevin."

Looking up at me he said, "Anything is possible. Let's just take our mind off things tonight. The nurse better hurry up or we're leaving without that damn test. We can take an Uber to the room and my brother can take me to pick up our cars tomorrow."

"Tasha will be back she can drop us off," I told him.

"Whichever is fastest once we can leave this place. I hate hospitals and I don't want to be here one minute longer than I have to," Monty said.

"Me either. I just want to go to sleep and wake up from this bad dream," I told him and put my head on his shoulder. I was still on his lap.

"It's going to be ok baby," Monty told me softly. "I'm going to make sure everything's ok. I got you now."

His words made me feel better. I leaned down and kissed him again. Hearing the door to the hospital room open, I looked up assuming that the nurse was finally back. Imagine my shock when I saw Kevin standing in the door and looking at Monty and I kiss!

"I came to see if you were alright after I found out our house caught fire. You didn't bother to call and let me know anything. Now I see why," he said calmly yet sounded disgusted.

Embarrassed, I didn't know what to say. It hurt me to keep hurting him but he was the one who filed divorced and refused to give me another chance. What more could I do?

"I was going to let you know tomorrow. Everything happened so fast that I wasn't thinking," I told him.

"It happened fast but you can call your fucking lover but not your husband who bought the damn house! You've lost your damn mind! That's why you don't need custody of the kids! Your only focus is on him!" Kevin got louder.

Standing up from Monty's lap, I got in Kevin's face. "You know damn well that I love my kids! The damn house caught fire! We could have died! Sorry that I didn't call your ass! Now get the fuck out of here! I'll call you tomorrow, so you'll know where to drop my babies off!" I yelled right back at his ass.

"Bitch, my kids are staying with me. There's no house to drop them to," he told me as he stared me in my face angrily. "This nigga dick got your mind so gone! You probably left the damn stove on in the house. You're too careless for my kids. Slut bitch!"

He tried to walk out after saying that to me but I wasn't having it. No way was he going to come in here and flip things on me. Hearing him call me all those names hurt my heart. "Who the fuck you calling a slut bitch? Fuck you!" I told him walking behind him. He turned around to face me again.

"I'm calling my whore ass wife a bitch!" he said. I knew he was hurt but he had a lot of nerve. I was hurt and angry too and I was tired of him treating me like I wasn't shit. Not even thinking, I spit in his face. I'd been through too much to keep letting him disrespect me. After wiping the spit from his face, he pushed me back so hard that I landed on my ass on the floor.

Before I could get up, Monty jumped from his seat and punched Kevin. They started fighting and punching each other right there in the hospital room. Finally, getting up from the floor, I saw them going hard at each other. Monty was punching Kevin but Kevin was taking those hits like they were nothing and he grabbed Monty and put him in a headlock. Not knowing what else to do, I jumped on Kevin's back and started hitting him so that he would let Monty go.

It wasn't long before the nurse came in and saw the commotion. We'd knock the phone and lamp down in the room. The nurse ran out and I could hear her calling for security. Kevin knocked me off of his back and I landed on the floor again. Monty had gotten loose from his grip by now and they were fighting hard again. Staring at them, I couldn't move. They were really punching and fighting each other hard. The hospital room was a mess.

"Please stop!" I screamed at them as loud as I could with tears in my eyes. I was so thankful when security came rushing into the room! There was no way in hell this night could get any worse!

CHAPTER 7

TASHA

Ty and I headed towards Nitra's room. I had some clothes for her and we were going to take her back with us to stay. It had taken a while to calm mama down but she finally soaked in the bathtub and laid down. In the morning, she would have a lot to figure out. Nitra had a lot of things to figure out too. We would all figure it out together. They both were there for me during my rough patches with Ty and I was going to be there for them.

Nearing the room, we heard yelling and commotion. What the fuck was going on? Pushing the room door open, the scene was unbelievable. There was a security guy holding Kevin. Another security guy was holding Monty. Judging by the blood on Kevin's lip and the blood under Monty's nose, it was obvious they had been fighting. The chair was turned over. The hospital bed wasn't in normal position. There was a lamp on the floor.

Searching the room for Nitra, I finally spotted her with her back against the wall. She was fully dressed but her hair was very disheveled. We'd brushed it down earlier. "What the hell is going on?" I asked her.

"Kevin came in here with the fuck shit," she said. "He called me all kinds of names and I spit on him. He pushed me and they started fighting."

"Oh my God," I said.

"We have to call the police," security was saying to the nurse.

"Please don't," Nitra told them. "We're all leaving now. Monty and I are fine. We don't need that last test. Just let us all leave and I promise you won't see us again."

"Ma'am, y'all tore the hospital room up. We have to call and report this. You have to pay for the damages," the nurse said. It was evident that she was angry.

"He shouldn't have brought his ass in my sister's room," I said while pointing at Kevin. "He wasn't invited and he only wanted to cause trouble."

"I was checking on her after I heard about the fire," Kevin said. "It was wrong that she didn't notify me of the fire.

It's my damn house too. I lost a lot of things too!" He was still angry but I could tell that he tried his best to disguise it.

"Why the hell would she call you? You're being petty as hell these days! Everything that transpired between you guys wasn't right but you know damn well she's a good mother!" My voice showed anger at him. Kevin had always been a pretty good guy but he was acting like a bitch lately. She was wrong for cheating but that was no reason to try to get full custody of my niece and nephew.

One of the bigger security guys spoke, "Look! You all need to shut up now or I'll make sure you all go to jail! Everyone just leave the hospital now! Quietly!"

Ty grabbed me by the arm and walked over and grabbed Nitra's hand. He gave us a look telling us to shut up and he quickly walked us out of the hospital room. We quickly made our way the elevators. Nobody said anything until we were in the elevator riding down.

"Y'all need to stay calm," Ty told us. "All that commotion in a public hospital is ludicrous! You all are actually lucky that they didn't call the police!"

"I know," Nitra said. "Everything is falling apart." Tears formed in her eyes and the elevator opened to the main floor.

"It's going to be ok sis," I told her while I took her hand and we all walked to the parking deck.

"What about Monty? I can't leave him," she said, looking back toward the hospital entrance.

"Sis, he can handle himself. He'll call you but right now you need to get out of here and get some rest and peace."

She nodded her head in agreement and got in the car. Ty drove us home.

CHAPTER 8

SANDY

We were sitting inside Lee's hotel room. We'd found a nice hotel that was an hour away from town. He convinced me to stay the night and rest before driving back in town by myself. Frazzled by the events of the day, I agreed. We went to a late-night Walmart to grab some underwear, pajamas, jeans, T-shirts, drinks and snacks.

I'd just gotten out of the shower. I was wearing a long cotton dress pajamas. Lee was sitting on the bed. He looked worried. For some reason, I actually felt sorry for him.

"Lee, I'll just give you the money," I told him. "If something happened to you, I wouldn't be able to live with myself. Lea needs you. Besides, it was money you gave me anyway."

Shaking his head, he said, "No. I want you to keep that money for you and Lea. You deserve every dime and more. I know what I got to do."

"What do you got to do? Look, I don't need you getting into any trouble. I'll still have a good chunk of money left after paying your debt. Let me help you please."

He looked up at me, "After everything I put you through, you're still willing to help me? You're so wonderful. I can't believe that I took you for granted. But, I can't take the money from you. I'm going to find that bitch Lisa and then I'm going to get back the money she stole and more!"

"What?" I asked him. "How are you going to find her? It would be dangerous going against her with her family."

"No one will know what happened," he told me. "Besides, they don't fuck with her like that anyway. She's stolen from them too; they just can't kill her because she's blood."

"Baby, don't get involved in no shit like that! I said that I'll give you the money. I'll still be straight in the money department. No worries! No need to go around getting into more trouble," I pleaded with him. I sat next to him on the bed so that he knew that I was serious.

"I can't let that bitch get away with taking my shit. She knew they would be after me for this! The bitch wanted me dead and she got me fucked up!" Lee spat. This was a side of Lee that I'd never seen before. He was sounding ruthless. The sound of his voice and the look on his face made me nervous, so I decided to be quiet on the subject. I would wait until he was calm and had time to think.

Rubbing his back, I calmed him down a bit. His breathing became normal. He'd been through so much tonight. Shit, I'd been through so much dealing with Tasha and her family drama. I just wanted to rest.

"Let's get some rest," I told him.

"Ok," he said while nodding. Turning to look at me, Lee leaned in and kissed me. After everything this man had put me through, it still felt good to kiss him. Maybe I was just lonely. Whatever it was, I didn't care. Tonight, I needed love and affection.

As we kissed, he lifted up my nightgown. "Take this shit off," he told me.

Smiling, I quickly lifted the gown over my head and threw it on the floor. Lee started to devour my breasts. His warm lips felt so good. While he licked my breasts, he used his fingers to play with my pussy. The sound of my moaning was all you could hear in the room. Within minutes, his tongue made its way to my vagina. His tongue French kissed my clit and it felt so damn good. The way he licked and twirled his tongue in and out my pussy made my feel like I was in heaven. He wouldn't come up for air as he continued to lick and please my pussy. Finally, I couldn't take no more and I screamed loudly with pleasure as I came in his mouth. He licked up every drop of cum.

Watching as he took off his clothes, I waited for him to climb on top of me. Once he was undressed, he just stared at me and smiled. "What you smiling bout?" I asked him.

"You. You think you're going to get some of this dick?" he said, smirking.

Not knowing what to say, I must have looked confused.

"I just wanted to taste that sweet pussy," he said. "Now you can go to sleep. I'm going to shower."

Laughing, I shook my head. Oh, so he didn't want to fuck? Shit, that was cool! I'd gotten my nut. I threw one of the pillows at him jokingly. He turned around and smiled then went into the bathroom to shower. Truly exhausted, I closed my eyes and went fast asleep.

CHAPTER 9

MISSY

It was getting very late and the sun would be up in a couple of hours. Therefore, I needed to hurry up. Standing in a wooded area many miles away from home, I used the shovel to finish covering up the hole that I'd dug earlier. I'd stripped off all the clothes that I wore so it wouldn't trace me back to the fire. I changed into my workout clothes that I always left in the car. I decided to bury everything that I wore that night along with other things. When I was done, I drove down the highway and headed home. Thoughts of the fire and events that happened after the fire were in my head. The things that happened in the last 24 hours were unbelievable. How could I go so far? I thought to myself.

Later, I finally pulled up to my house. It was a relief to be home. Unlocking the door, I walked into the safety of my home. It was a blessing my kids were with my mom. Stripping off my clothes, I put them in a plastic shopping bag. Walking to my bathroom, I turned the shower on and made sure the water was nice and warm before getting in. It had to be at least an hour that I stayed in the shower. Getting out of the shower, I dried off and put on my robe.

Exhausted from being up all day and night, I lay in my bed and went fast asleep.

~

A few hours later, I was awakened by knocking on the door and the doorbell ringing. It took me a minute to get up and focus. Nervously, I went to the door wondering who the hell could be knocking like that. Looking through the peephole, I saw Monty's sister. We'd always been close. I'd been avoiding her and his entire family since the breakup. Facing them meant facing the facts of my life.

"Hey," I said sleepily when I opened the door.

"Hey girl," Shonda, Monty's sister said coming in the door. "Have you heard from Monty? Our brother Dez just told me that he was in the hospital for smoke inhalation. He said something about a fire. I don't know the details. You know Monty and Dez are so damn secretive when it comes to me."

"Fire? Smoke inhalation? What happened?" I asked her, hoping that I didn't sound suspicious and nervous. I'd been wondering all night if they had gotten out of the house. In the spur of the moment, I didn't care if they'd died or not. But now I found myself relieved to know that my baby daddy was still alive. Secretly, I hoped that bitch was hurt real bad.

"I don't know what happened. Dez just called to tell me and then he told me he would tell me more later," Shonda said. "Where are my niece and nephew? Auntie wants to give them a hug."

"They're still with my mom girl. They'll be coming home tonight."

"You're still depressed and moping over Monty? Fuck him. He was dead wrong. Find you some new dick and I bet his ass will be jealous," she told me. I liked Shonda because she treated me like a friend and didn't take her brother's side like most bitches did.

"I know. I'm good," I told her. "I'm slowly getting back to me."

"Shit you better," Shonda said. "These niggas ain't shit. Start doing like K-Michelle said in that song, 'Love 'Em All'."

Looking at Shonda, I burst out laughing. She was crazy as hell. Knowing that I needed to take my mind off of things, I welcomed Shonda to spend the day with me.

"Girl, I got some weed and some drink," I told her. "If you ain't busy, let's chill until your niece and nephew come home."

"That's fine with me!" Shonda said. She was always ready to turn up in some kind of way. It was a wonder that she didn't have kids yet. She was still young though. At only 24, she was 4 years younger than me. I guess everyone didn't have to have kids as early as I did.

"Order some Chinese delivery," I told her as I went to grab the weed out of my room. "You know we're going to be hungry soon."

"Okkk!" Shonda said while she danced. Shaking my head, I laughed at her crazy ass.

CHAPTER 10

NITRA

After arriving to Tasha's house, I jumped in the shower in the guest bedroom. It was a blessing that Tasha's guest bedrooms had their own bath. That way, I didn't have to come out for anything. Time for me was much needed. What the fuck was going on in my life? Drying off, I looked at myself in the mirror. Who was this person? Who was Nitra? What was I going to do with my life now that Kevin wouldn't be in it anymore? There was so many things that I needed to figure out for myself but yet I couldn't stay away from Monty. Was he meant to be in my life? Did I really love him?

Thinking of Monty, I grabbed my cell phone. Before dialing his number, I noticed that there were 3 missed calls from him. I'd put my phone on silent at the hospital earlier. As if on cue, my phone lit up and it was Monty calling again.

"Hey," I answered.

"Hey baby," he said. "I've been calling you ever since I left the hospital. Thankfully, they let us go without calling the police. They just made sure we left separately. I'm so sorry about everything that happened. I just couldn't take him talking to you like that."

"I know baby," I said, softening up. There was something about him that made my heart flutter. "I'm at Tasha's house. I'm going to stay here tonight and get my thoughts together and get some rest. Baby, someone set my house on fire. Do you think someone could have really been trying to hurt me?"

"Unfortunately, yes. The way Kevin acted tonight it could very well have been him," Monty said. "Let me come get you so I know that you're safe with me."

"No. My Mom is here. Some things went on with her tonight too. I just want to rest and see what's going on with her in the morning. She needs me. I'll call you tomorrow afternoon. Get you some rest too bae."

"I can't rest without you," Monty told me. "Baby, so much has happened. I need to be with you tonight."

"Monty, I want to be with you too but I'm exhausted. My life is falling apart. My Mom just got married and now it may be over. My kids and I lost everything in a fire. My ex is trying to take custody. My lover and my ex just tore down the hospital room fighting. If I had been with my Mom tonight, maybe I could have helped her. We wouldn't have had to escape from a damn fire either!" My voice went from sounding sad and frustrated to angry. Before he could respond, I burst out crying.

"Calm down baby. I hate to hear you crying. I'm on the way," Monty told me. Though I was balled up on the bed, the phone was to my ear. I tried calming down my sobs.

"No baby," I told him. "I just want to sleep." Looking down at the phone, I noticed that he'd hung up. Getting comfortable on the bed, I put the phone beside me on the nightstand. My body must have been tired because within minutes, I was sleep.

I was awakened out of my sleep by the vibrating sounds of my phone on the nightstand. "Hello," I said answering the phone.

"Baby, I'm about to pull up. Come open the door in 5 minutes," Monty said on the other end of the phone.

"Pull up where? Monty, I told you that I was tired. You shouldn't have come."

"And I told you that I couldn't sleep without you. Baby, I'm worried about you," he told me. He sounded genuinely concerned so I softened up.

"Ok bae," I told him and added, "But you have to leave real early in the morning and let me spend the day with my Mom."

"Of course," he told me.

Getting up, I tiptoed to the door to let him in. The house was quiet and everyone was sleeping. Grabbing him by the hand, I led him to the room that I was occupying. Once we entered the room, he hugged me tight. He felt so good and warm in my arms. Finally loosening our hug, he kissed me. Though I was tired, I didn't fuss as he lay me down on my back and took off my clothes. He started licking my nipples and the sensation made my pussy wet. Once he started sticking his finger in and out of my pussy, I couldn't help but moan softly. He continued licking my nipples and played with my pussy using his finger. It felt so good that I started throwing my pussy back to his finger.

Monty took his finger out of my pussy and put it in my mouth. I sucked all my juices from his finger. He moved his lips down to my pussy. He stuck his tongue in and out of my hole. He knew this made me go insane. "Damn baby," I told him while moaning. He didn't respond. He just kept licking on my pussy. Just when I thought I was about to cum, he stopped licking. By this time, I was craving his dick. Between my legs was like a river and I was ready for him to jump in.

Knowing what I wanted, Monty took off his clothes and slowly stuck his dick in my pussy. He started moaning after feeling the warmness of my wet pussy. Staring in my eyes, he kissed me passionately. We made love until we fell asleep.

CHAPTER 11

TASHA

Feeling Ty get out of the bed, I opened my eyes. The bright lights from the window let me know it was well into morning. Looking at the clock, I noticed it was after 9:00 a.m. It was a Sunday and the kids were still with Terry so I could lie around for a while. Remembering the events of the night before, it dawned on me that my mom and Nitra were here. I needed to get up.

"Good morning baby," Ty told me as he walked into the bathroom.

"Good morning," I replied while stretching and getting up out of the bed joining him in the bathroom, he was brushing his teeth. We had two sinks so I went to my sink and washed up too.

"I'll grab breakfast for you and the ladies," Ty told me. "Then I'll run some errands and give you some privacy."

"Thanks baby," I told him. "I'm so lucky to have you. Thank you for being with me."

Ty smiled and said, "Thank you for being my woman. I love you with all my heart."

"I love you too," I told him and kissed him passionately. He got dressed and left out. I slipped on some jeans and a tank top. Putting my slides on, I went to check on Mom. She wasn't in her room. Heading down the stairs, I laughed and shook my head. She was probably up cooking breakfast or something knowing her. She never liked being catered to.

The kitchen was dark when I entered it. Looking in my living room, I didn't see Mom in there either. My house was big so she had to be somewhere in here. I decided to see if Nitra was awake. The fire and everything that happened yesterday kept running through my mind. She was sure to have had a sleepless night. Reaching the room that Nitra was sleeping in, I knocked. "Sis? You up yet?" I asked her.

There seemed to be movement in the room so she must have been up. Wanting to make sure she was ok, I turned the knob and walked into the room. My mouth opened in shock when I saw her and Monty on the bed naked and having sex.

Monty was on his back and Nitra was on top riding him. His hands were playing with her nipples.

She jumped off of him and shrieked when she saw me. After a few seconds of standing there frozen, I finally turned around and ran out of the room. I ran back to my room. For some reason, I started laughing as I sat on my bed. Nitra's ass was fucking. With all the shit she had going on, leave it to her to make time for dick. I didn't blame her though. It was too strange seeing her and Monty naked and fucking. For years I'd seen him with Missy.

Remembering my mission of finding my Mom, I searched the rest of my house to no avail. She'd rode with Bernard here yesterday so she didn't have her car with her. Where could she have gone? Opening my front door, I went out on the porch. The sun was shining and it was a beautiful day. Ty drove up in the driveway. He looked sexy as hell as he got out of the car with bags in his hand. My stomach growled at that moment. It must have smelled the food.

"Hey bae," I said to him and kissed his lips when he walked up to me. I held open the front door for him as he walked in with the food.

"Hey. I went to the breakfast bar that you like. I got everything. We got pancakes, grits, eggs, sausage, bacon, biscuits and more. Go get your Mom and Nitra," he told me.

"I don't know where my mom is. I've been searching the house for her since you left. And Nitra snuck company in last night. Unknowingly, I walked in on them having sex."

"Really?" Ty asked. He started laughing. "Sis just needed to get some stress off of her chest."

Laughing with him, I shook my head. "Well, I'm hungry. The food will be here when they are ready to eat. We can eat now."

Ty and I started eating when my phone rang. The call said ANONYMOUS. I usually didn't answer phone numbers that I couldn't see but thinking of my mom made me answer.

"Hello?" I answered.

"You better do something with your damn mama!" It was my cousin Lacy screaming into the phone.

"What?" I asked her. This bitch had much nerve to call me after everything that her mom did.

"Aunt Karen is outside my mom's house. She's trying to get her to come outside and talk. She needs to go. I don't want to call the police on my aunt so I'm trying to be nice by calling you. I know yesterday was crazy but she needs to leave," Lacy said to me with an attitude. "I'm on the way over there now."

At least now I knew where my mom went, I thought to myself. That lady was crazy. "I'm on the way over there," I told Lacy then hung up.

"What happened baby?" Ty asked me.

"Mom's crazy ass is in front of Aunt Kathy's door telling her to come outside. That was Lacy. I'm on the way around there."

Ty shook his head and laughed. "I'm marrying into a crazy family," he told me. "Come on. I'll take you to get her."

"Thanks baby," I said while making sure the food was covered. Ty and I left out the door to head over to Aunt Kathy's house. Sitting in the passenger seat, I looked over at him as he pulled out of our driveway. Ty was the love of my life. Craziness was in my life ever since he'd met me. I was grateful that he still stuck with me through everything.

CHAPTER 12

SANDY

The next morning, I woke up and turned over to see if Lee was awake. To my surprise, he wasn't in the bed. Getting up, I went into the bathroom to see if he was there. Seeing no sign of him, I decided to wash up. Where could he be? After gathering my things, I looked at my cell phone. There were no missed calls or messages from him. Maybe he was getting breakfast? But how would he get there when I drove? My car keys were still here.

I called his phone but he didn't answer. Not knowing what was going on, I decided to head home. My keys were in my hand as I reached my car in the parking lot. Just as I was about to get into the car, some guy walked up on me and grabbed my arm.

"Hey, what the fuck are you doing?" I asked him while jerking away from him.

"Keep calm and I won't harm you," he told me. He made sure to show me the gun in his waist. Scared as hell, I didn't know what the hell was going on!

"What do you want from me? You can take my purse," I told him while handing him my purse. It had some cash and credit cards in it. Nothing was worth my life.

"That won't be necessary," he told me. "What you need to do is come back to this parking lot tomorrow morning at 10. Banks will be back open then. You need to have $50,000 in cash to give me, if you don't want me to kill your baby's daddy. If you get the police involved, he's dead." He walked off quickly yet smoothly. Nervously, I jumped into my car and drove off.

~

Over an hour later, I arrived at my house. Now I knew where Lee was. But how had they gotten him? Did he leave the room to get something and get snatched up? My heart couldn't take anymore. First, hell broke loose with Tasha's mom and Nitra. Now, I had to deal with this. Should I give them the money? I didn't want anything to happen to Lee but what if they did something to me? There was no way that I could do this alone. Tasha was dealing with too much already, so I didn't want to get her and Ty involved. What should I do?

Needing to think, I went to my stash of loud and rolled up a joint. There was no way that I could risk something happening to Lee. Tomorrow morning, I would get the money from where it was stashed and meet the guy. He didn't hurt me today, so maybe he wouldn't hurt me tomorrow. So many thoughts went through my head as I sat and smoked. The ringing doorbell took me out of my thoughts.

Peeping through the peep hole, I saw that it was my mom and Lea.

"Mom, you didn't call and say you were on the way," I told her.

"It shouldn't matter if I'm bringing your child home," she told me. "You been smoking that stuff in this house?"

"No mom," I said, annoyed. "Mom can you keep Lea and take her to school in the morning? I have some important things to do."

"I have some things to do too," she told me. She gave Lea a hug and stared at me sternly. "Bye," she told me dryly then left.

"Mama, what you been doing?" Lea asked me, giggling.

Forcing a smile, I said, "Nothing sweetie. Did you have fun this weekend?"

"Yes," she told me. I grabbed her hand and led her towards her room to put up her bags. She told me all about her weekend as I looked at her and smiled. There was no way that I could let anything happen to her father. She loved us both so much and I couldn't stand to see my little girl's heart broken. It was worth the risk to help Lee.

CHAPTER 13

NITRA

Embarrassed wasn't a strong enough word for how I felt when Tasha walked in on me riding Monty. Why the hell didn't her ass knock? Monty and I woke up making love. He was planning on leaving afterwards. Never did I imagine Tasha walking in on us. Once she left out of the room, we got dressed quickly and Monty left. He told me that he wanted me to stay with him at a hotel tonight and I agreed that I would.

After showering and changing, I went into the kitchen. There was a bunch of food spread out on the table. I fixed me a plate. The food was warm, so Tasha and Mom couldn't be too far. Eating, I braced myself for us all to have a talk. I'd devoured my food and they still hadn't come into the kitchen. Wondering where they were, I walked around the house.

"Mom?" I said loudly, so that she could hear me wherever she was. "Tasha? Sis?"

I sure hoped that they hadn't left because of the sex thing. Deciding to focus on other things, I wondered how my house looked after the fire. There was so much that I needed to do. I would have to get a copy of the police report and call the insurance company. Tomorrow was Monday, so I would do everything then. I planned on getting my babies from Kevin tomorrow too. My kids would live wherever I lived. Where was I going to live? That was a good question. Most likely, I would live with Mom. If she and Bernard were having issues, she could use the company. My babies always cheered her up. Tasha had a big house but her and Ty were just getting things on track and I didn't want to impose on their privacy.

Calling Tasha's phone, I was angry when she didn't answer. Where the hell were they? What the hell was going on?

CHAPTER 14

TASHA

Arriving to Aunt Kathy's house, I noticed that Mom was standing in front of her car. She must have caught an Uber from my house to her house to get her car. That lady is so sneaky, I thought to myself as Ty parked behind her and turned off the engine. Before he could shut the car off good, I jumped out of the car.

"Mom," I said. She turned toward me. "I know you're hurt and what Aunt Kathy did was fucked up but please let's just go back to my house. Fuck her and this raggedy ass house. We all know she's always been jealous of you."

Mom looked so hurt. She'd always been a tough lady but I could tell that this situation really hurt. She'd finally chosen to settle down and her sister sucks her new husband's dick! That shit is wild! Grabbing Mom's hand, I was annoyed when I heard Lacy's voice behind me.

"Bitch, my mama ain't ever been jealous of your mom! I heard what the hell you said!" Lacy was standing near her mother's porch.

"Who the fuck is you calling a bitch?" I asked her. "You're a professional side hoe!" Ty jumped out of the car when he saw me walk toward Lacy. He must have known that I was going to slap that hoe! He pulled me back. He held my arm with his right hand and at the same time he held my mom's hand with his left hand. My baby was trying to keep control of the situation because he knew that I would take it there.

The commotion made Aunt Kathy come outside finally. "Y'all just get from in front of my door!" she yelled. "It's not my fault your husband can't keep his hands off of me! You fucked Steven years ago, so now you know how it feels!"

"Bitch! That was high school!" My mom yelled. Mom ran up on the porch where her sister was standing and started punching her. She had her in a headlock by the time I could get on the porch.

Lacy grabbed my mom's arm and said, "Get off my mom, Auntie!"

Seeing the little bitch touch my mom made me see red. I boxed Lacy in her face and grabbed her by her hair. She started crying and screaming, "Stop Tasha! Let me go!"

"Bitch, don't ever touch my mom again!" I told her and then I pushed her so hard that she fell off of the porch. Looking back, Ty was grabbing my mom because she was still fighting Aunt Kathy. By this time, Aunt Kathy's wig had come off. In all the mess, I laughed.

"Help me get your mom!" Ty told me. Obeying him, I grabbed my mom and quickly escorted her off of the porch. Ty had helped Aunt Kathy up and was saying sorry. Lacy was off the ground and looked like she wanted to try something again but she knew better. Ty promised them that we were leaving and convinced them to go in the house. Handing me his keys he said, "Drive your mom home in my car and I'll take her car. The keys are still in the ignition."

"Thanks baby," I said. He just shook his head and walked off. I know he was disappointed in my fighting…again…but I couldn't let that tramp talk to my mom like that. Cranking up Ty's car, I pulled off. Mom sat quietly as she straightened up her clothes and checked in the mirror to make sure her hair was straight. No wonder I was so quick to pop off. I got it from my mama!

CHAPTER 15

NITRA

I'd drifted off to sleep on the sofa. Hearing the front door to Tasha's house open woke me up. I saw Mom, Tasha and Ty walk in.

"Where y'all been?" I asked.

Tasha just shook her head. "Your mom went to fight Aunt Kathy," she told me.

"Wait! What?" Did I just hear them right?

Everyone sat in the living area where I was. Mom sat near me while Tasha and Ty sat on the opposite sofa.

"I forgot you don't know what happened because of the fire," Tasha told me. Then, she filled me in on everything. I was disgusted to find out what Aunty Kathy and Bernard did. Mom had been through so much!

"Oh no, I'm so sorry Mom," I told her and hugged her. "Did you beat that bitch ass? She's always been jealous of you!"

"Right!" Tasha said. "Yes, she beat her ass and I beat Lacy's ass."

"It's nothing to brag about," Ty told her.

"I know baby," she said. "It's just that seeing my mom hurt makes me hurt."

"I understand," he told her and kissed her.

"I'll be ok," Mom said. "I just wish that I wouldn't have wasted time signing marriage license and now I have to file for divorce."

"Did Bernard call?" I asked her. "What did he say? Not that it matters either way."

"Yes, but I didn't answer. He's been texting. He says he just wants to have one talk with me. He says there are some things that he really needs to tell me," she said.

"Are you going to talk to him?" I asked her.

"No. I'm done. If I saw him now, I would kill him. He needs to stay far away from me," Mom said. If he knew what I knew, he would do just that. Mom was no joke.

The room was quiet for a few seconds when Tasha said, "Nitra, how are you doing? Your house caught fire and you lost everything."

Feeling the tears come, I just shook my head. "I don't know what I'm going to do sis. Monty and Kevin fought at the hospital because Kevin was being disrespectful and hateful. He's telling me that he's keeping the kids. Monty's thinking Kevin set the fire."

"I said the same thing!" Tasha said. "Kevin probably did set that fire. And what damn kids does he think he's keeping? Y'all haven't gone to court for custody so you're still the one with primary custody. As a matter of fact, we need to go get them now."

Why hadn't I thought about that? "You're right. I was going to let them stay one more night and let him take them to school but I've changed my mind. My car didn't catch fire. I just have to pick it up and I can buy them a few things to wear for the next week or so. Since his ass wants to deal with court then that's what we'll do."

"Hell yea," Tasha said. "I'll take you to get your car. Call and tell him to either meet us somewhere with the kids or we'll call the police. I don't trust his ass anyway.

"I'll call him. First, take me to see the house damage and get my car," I told her.

"Ok," Tasha said.

"Mom, do you want to come?" I asked her.

"No. I'm going to lie down. I promise that I won't disappear this time," she said.

"You better not," I told her while laughing.

~

Tasha and I pulled up to my house. It looked a burnt mess! Luckily, I always parked my car on the street and not in the driveway. Tasha parked and we both got out. Yellow tape was everywhere. The left side of the house seemed to have the most damage. It must have been where the fire started. Part of the roof was burned off and gone. Thinking about everything that I lost and knowing that I could have lost my life in the fire made me break down and cry. I was standing in front of a skeleton of my home. Technically, I was homeless.

Tasha came and rubbed my back. "It's going to be ok sis. Insurance will replace everything. Thank God, you're safe and the kids weren't in there. That's what's important. We'll replace the materials."

Feeling better, I nodded my head. She was absolutely right. "You're right sis. Thanks for always being here for me."

"Of course," Tasha said. "Shit, you've always been there for my bullshit. Even as little girls you've had my back. It's my turn. My home is your home. You and the kids can stay as long as you want."

"Thanks for the offer," I told her. "I'll definitely stay the next few days until I figure things out."

"It's whatever you want to do," she told me. Smiling through my tears, I finally felt better. Now, I just needed to call Kevin and let him know that I was getting the kids tonight and taking them to school tomorrow. I would tell them what happened to our house fragilely.

Pulling out my cell phone, I dialed Kevin's number.

"Hello?" he answered with an attitude.

"Kev, I want to make this quick. I don't want to argue or have any issues with you," I told him.

"What do you want?" he asked me.

"I want you to bring the kids to Tasha's house later. They need to be with me and I need to be with them. I'll have to tell them about our house."

"I'm keeping the kids," he growled at me. "They're not going to be staying pillow to post with you until you figure things out."

"Bitch nigga, my kids will never have to live pillow to post. Insurance will pay for our house and in the meantime, I'll find a place to live until it's repaired. For now, my kids and I will be staying at Tasha's house. She has plenty of space. My mother also has a nice house nigga, so don't ever say no shit about me living pillow to post!" He had me angry. This man was treating me like we hadn't spent most of my damn life together!

Tasha looked at me and said, "Did that bitch nigga say you're pillow to post? Put the phone on speaker!" I put the phone on speaker as she requested. I knew she would go off on him.

"Kevin!" Tasha yelled into the phone. "You got a lot of nerve how you're acting! We're all supposed to be family! Your house burned down. It was your kids' home! But you choose to be an asshole just because you're hurt and bitter. I'm really starting to believe that you set the fire! Bring my niece and nephew to my house in the next hour or I will be calling the police and telling them my suspicions!"

"Suspicions?" he asked. "Why would I set my own house on fire? After getting custody, the courts are going to let me keep the house anyway. I'm the money maker."

Still on speaker, I yelled, "You're the money maker and that's how you wanted it! Therefore, you will have to pay the bills and I stay in the house with my kids! Don't fucking play with me!"

"Y'all don't play with me! You know damn well I wouldn't set the house on fire!" he yelled.

"We don't know shit!" Tasha yelled into the phone before he could say anything.

"Bring me my kids Kevin! Please!" I practically begged him. I was exhausted and I just wanted my babies.

"I'll bring them at 5," he said, finally giving in. I guess talk of him setting the fire scared him. "But, we need to talk."

"I'm not in a talking mood!" I told him. "Just bring my babies and we'll talk sometime next week. Our house caught fire! I have too much to take care of. I don't need your bullshit right now."

"Ok," he said then hung up. Tasha and I headed back to her house. I followed her in my car.

CHAPTER 16

MISSY

As I opened my eyes, I could feel my head pounding. Sitting up from the sofa, I saw Shonda asleep on the other coach. We'd been smoking and drinking and must have passed out. Getting up was hard because of my headache. I grabbed my phone and saw that it was just 6 in the evening. Mom would be bringing the kids any minute.

"Shonda! Wake up!" I told her and shook her lightly. She slowly started to wake up. My doorbell started ringing and I knew who it was. Opening the door, my mother and my kids stood there.

"Damn you look a mess!" my mother told me. She looked disgusted.

"I'm just waking up Mom. I have a migraine. Hey babies!" I said as I hugged the kids. They smiled and gave me hugs. By now, Shonda had gotten up.

"Hey Auntie babies!" Shonda told them walking towards the door.

"Hey Auntie!" they said running to her. They loved their Auntie. She always spent time with them and bought them things.

Mom just stood staring at me disgustingly.

"Thanks for everything Mom," I told her while trying to ignore her stares. "I'll call you tomorrow."

"Ok," she said. "Good night babies!" she told the kids and she left. She wanted to say more but I knew that she didn't because Shonda and the kids were around.

The kids told Shonda and me about their weekend and then Shonda left. I gave them their baths and tucked them in. Mom had already fed them. They had school tomorrow. Seeing my kids gave me peace. It reminded me of what could happen if anyone found out about the fire. What the hell was I thinking? So much had happened in the last couple of days. When I got to my bedroom, I got on my knees and prayed hard. I asked God for forgiveness of everything that I'd done in the past few days.

CHAPTER 17

SANDY

The next morning, I got up early. I got dressed and I took Lea to school. After dropping her off, I went to my stash and took out the $50,000. I still had over $40,000 left so it wouldn't leave me broke. It wasn't worth Lee dying over. Wanting to call Tasha, I changed my mind. I would call her later on. She hadn't tried calling me, so I know that she was tied up anyway. She didn't need to know about this situation.

At 10:00, I arrived at the spot and looked around. I was nervous. He wasn't going to get the money upfront. He was going to have to release Lee first. A few minutes had passed when I saw a black SUV pulled up beside me. The windows were tinted and it made me nervous. We were at the end of the parking lot away from all the other cars. Stepping out of my car empty handed, I made sure to leave the bag with the money hidden in the car.

A guy opened the driver's door to the car. "Where's the money?" he asked me.

"Where's Lee?" I asked him. I was nervous as hell but you wouldn't know it by my demeanor.

"Girl, you think you're tough or something?" he asked me as he stepped out of the car.

"No," I told him. "I just feel like fair is fair."

The guy shook his head. "You're lucky you're pretty and I only came for my money. Or else, I would teach you a lesson about not obeying orders."

"Where is Lee?" I asked again.

The guy looked agitated. "I told your ass that he's in the backseat." Opening the back door slightly, he let me peep in. Lee was in the last row of the SUV tied up by his hands and legs. He had duck tape over his mouth. Looking at him made me realize how serious the situation was.

"Now give me the damn money bitch. We should have been gone by now," the guy said.

"I don't have to be a bitch," I told him as I headed to get the money out of my car. "Some of y'all men can be so damn disrespectful."

"You're still talking shit like this is a game?" the guy said sounding agitated. "Hurry and get me the money before it gets ugly." He lightly shoved me in the back.

Remaining quiet, I opened the door to my car and grabbed the small bag where the money was. Silently, I prayed that all will go well and he would give up Lee as promised.

"Here you go. Can you let him go with me now please? Please?" I felt the need to say it again.

"Come sit in the truck while I untie him," he told me.

"No, I'll wait out here," I told him. Why would I want to get in the truck with him? I thought to myself.

"Get your ass in the truck," he said shoving me in the seat in front of Lee's. He started to untie Lee then he stopped. "You know what? Before I let y'all go, you're going to blow me off."

"What?" I asked. I reached for the door handle to get out but he grabbed my arm and slapped me hard. Holding my face, I didn't know what to do. We were in a truck with dark tint so no one could see even if they did come down this way. Screaming would be a big risk because he had a gun.

"This could have been over but you got to act like you're in control," the guy said. He was ugly with big bumps on his face. He wore shades and a hat but there was no hiding those ugly bumps. Lee moved around in the backseat as if to try to help in some way. The guy grabbed me by the neck with one hand and unzipped his pants with the other. I tried squirming out of his grip but wasn't successful.

"Now we're going to see if you know how to listen," he said. He pulled out his dick then took out his gun all with his left hand. His right hand still held my neck as he sat next to me on the seat. I could feel Lee's eyes looking behind us. "Suck my dick then you and him can go free. Disobey me or get smart and he's not going to make it."

Real fear set in. Was this really happening? Why didn't I just give him the money and trust that he would let Lee go? Tears slowly fell from my face but I was too scared to sniffle or make a sound. He moved my neck towards his dick and I felt like pure trash as I put my lips on his stink dick.

"Hurry up," he told me then he slapped the back of my head with his hand. Wanting to get it over with and get out of the situation, I began sucking his big black dick. He moved my head for me to the rhythm that he wanted me to go. I fought back tears and sucked as he quickly moved my head up and down his dick. The way he shoved my head back and forth hurt and his dick made me want to gag. Lee's movement was getting to be too much. It had to be hard for him to watch this. After what seemed like being tortured forever, the guy's dick swelled up in my mouth and I knew that he was about to cum. Trying to release my mouth from his dick, I wasn't in time because I could taste his nasty warm cum in my mouth. Finally, he let me come up for air and I could feel his cum draining from the sides of my mouth.

"Get in your car and I'll untie him," the guy told me. With a mouth and face full of cum, I hurried out of his car into my car. Grabbing napkins from the glove department, I spit up what was in my mouth and wiped my face. Humiliation was too light of a word for how I felt. Minutes later, Lee was being shoved out of the car and the truck pulled off. He quickly got in my car and I pulled off. Tears flooded my face as soon as I hit the gas and sped off. This weekend had gotten worse than I could have ever imagined.

CHAPTER 18

TASHA

It was Monday and all of our kids were off to school. Last night, Terry brought my kids back and Kevin did as promised and dropped off my niece and nephew. Nitra was in the kitchen sitting at the table on the phone. She'd been handling insurance business regarding her house all morning. Ty was working and Mom wanted to go home to her own house. Ty followed her over there so that he could change her locks so that Bernard couldn't get in.

The kids were shocked about the fire when we told them but to make them feel better we let them know that they would just have to get new and better things. I loved my niece and nephew as if they were my kids and my kids were so happy that they were staying with us for a while. I'm sure that we would have to get used to the noise all the time.

Hanging up the phone, Nitra looked worn out. "This shit is so sickening," she said. "An adjustor is going to call me and set up a time to go over all the losses in the house. The insurance coverage that we have covers paying a certain amount of rent to live somewhere else while they rebuild our house. I'm going to start looking for a place and we should be out in a few weeks."

"I'm not rushing you to get out," I let her know. "The kids love the company and so do I. Ty is working all the time and with me working at home, I need help with the baby. Thank God for Ty's cousin. She kept the baby this weekend with everything going on. She's bringing him back in a bit."

"She better bring my nephew back," Nitra said. "I miss him."

"Me too," I told her. "But it was nice not having to wake up in the middle of the night."

"You're a trip," she told me. "The detective called and said that it was definitely arson. They're investigating the property. Who would set my house on fire?"

"Kevin," I told her.

"No. I don't think that he did. He was mad that we accused him," she told me.

"He was so mad lately. I do think it was him. Who else could it have been?" I asked her.

"It could have been Missy," Nitra blurted out.

"Missy?" I asked. "I've known her for years. She gets crazy and does a lot of fucked up things but I don't think she would do that. Your kids could have been in the house. Kevin knew your kids weren't home because he had them."

She shook her head. "Missy is a possibility just as much as Kevin. Besides, last night I asked the kids if their dad took them to a babysitter or left them with someone this weekend and they said no. Saturday night, which is the night of the fire, they said they were home with Kevin watching a movie. They're small but they'll know if their dad wasn't around."

I nodded my head. Could it have been Missy?

"I'm pretty sure that it was some teenagers playing around and it went too far," she said.

"Could be," I said. For some reason, Kevin was still a suspect in my mind. But now, so was Missy.

~

A few hours later, Nitra left. I was pretty sure that she was going to meet Monty. She was so obsessed with him. They acted as if they were really in love. Maybe they were. Baby TJ was back and I was playing with him in the den. I'd missed my baby. Though I was supposed to be working from home, I hadn't opened my laptop today. Tomorrow, I planned on catching up on a few things.

I could hear someone turning the key in the front door, so I looked towards the entrance. Ty walked in looking worried.

"What's wrong baby?" I asked him. TJ looked up at his Dad and made some noise. He missed his dad. He started laughing and trying to talk. Seeing this made Ty smile and soften up. Grabbing TJ from me, he sat next to me.

"Latisha's cousin called me and said she's had Latisha's kids since Saturday. She was supposed to keep them until Sunday morning but she hasn't heard anything from her," Ty said.

"What? Where is Latisha?" I asked him.

"I just said that the cousin doesn't know," Ty said. He sounded agitated but I understood.

"Damn," I said. "I wonder what's going on and where the hell she is!"

"I don't know," Ty said. "But I told her cousin that I'll be picking up Tyvonna from school today. She can keep her cousin's son until she shows up. I'm keeping my daughter for good. I'm going to call my lawyer and file custody and report that she's missing in action. Tyvonna deserves better in life than a trifling mother!"

"You're right baby," I told him. "Teriana is going to be so happy to know that Tyvonna will be here all the time. She'll have a sister around. It's already a daycare in here with Nitra's kids so we'll be partying everyday."

Ty shook his head and smiled at me. I guess I sounded like a big kid. He dialed his lawyer and I sat beside him and rubbed his leg and back. He'd been here for me through everything so I was going to do the same for him.

CHAPTER 19

NITRA

The waitress seated me at the booth while I waited for Monty to show up. We were meeting for lunch. The kids were in school and I'd been running errands related to the house and fire all morning. I'd be receiving a check for living expenses in a couple of weeks so I was apartment hunting. I just needed a place for me and my kids until my house was finished getting remodeled. It would be a process. The police said they would let me know what their investigation finds out. They didn't have any suspects yet. Kevin and I were scheduled for court next week. He filed for temporary full custody of the kids because of my living arrangement. Instead of sympathizing, he saw the fire as yet another way to hurt me.

Monty walked in and I smiled. He'd been my shoulder through the process. He didn't like that I wasn't staying with him but he understood that I couldn't because of the kids. Sitting across from me he asked, "How was your day beautiful?"

"Stressful but productive," I told him. The waitress came over and we ordered lunch.

"That's good that it was productive. My day was crazy. Lil Monty's school called me to tell me that he was acting up the last couple of days. They tried calling Missy first but she hasn't been answering her phone," he said.

"Oh wow," I said. "Breakups are hard on kids too. Maybe you should go talk to him. Spend some time with him and his sister."

"I've been trying to contact Missy for the last couple of weeks but she's purposely not answering. I just wanted to give her space and time to heal. But, I'm feeling bad now. My kids need me," he said. He looked defeated. I'd never seen this worried side of Monty before. It made me feel bad for him.

"Why don't you go over there when the kids get out of school? Maybe she'll let you take them out to eat?" I suggested to him.

"I'll do that," he said. "Missy and I need to talk about custody and visitation. She likes to party so maybe she'll agree to me getting the kids on weekends. My sister Shonda and she are close. If she acts crazy, I'll get Shonda to convince her to let me get more time with the kids."

"That'll be good," I told him. Our food arrived and we ate lunch.

After we left the restaurant Monty asked, "Don't you have a couple of hours before you have to pick the kids up from school?"

"Yes," I told him. "I'll probably go to Tasha's and look online for apartments."

"Come to my house with me? I need some of you," he told me.

"Won't your brother be home?" I asked. I'd never been to his place that he shared with his brother. We use to always chill at my house or a hotel room.

"No, he's at work. It doesn't matter either way. I'm allowed company," he laughed.

"I know," I said. "It's just that I'd feel more comfortable doing the nasty without someone else in the house. It's crazy that I've never been to your place."

"Well, today is the day," he told me. "Follow me so you'll have your car."

"Ok," I told him and got in my car to follow him as requested. Part of me told me that I needed to slow down with Monty and deal with my divorce and Kevin before jumping into anything serious. But, there was a part of me that felt that Monty could be the one for me. He was very attentive. With Kevin, I used to practically beg for attention.

Shortly after, we pulled up to the apartments that Monty was sharing with his brother. He'd been staying here since the breakup and planned to get his own spot soon. The apartment complex was clean and seemed quiet. I parked next to him and got out and followed him to the apartment. Walking in, I could tell it was a bachelor pad. It had a big TV in the living room and a game console. He took my hand and led me to his bedroom. There were Queen sized mattresses on the floor and a TV sitting on the dresser. Other than that, the room was empty.

He sat on the bed so I sat beside him. For some reason, I felt so out of place. What was I doing in this room with him?

"Are you ok baby?" Monty asked me.

"No," I said, shaking my head. "My whole life is falling apart. I feel so helpless."

He grabbed me close to him and lie back on the bed so that I could lie on his chest. Our feet were still hanging off of the mattress.

"Baby, I know everything seems to be spiraling out of control. Sometimes life throws curveballs. You're going to slowly get back everything you lost in the fire. It's going to be better than before. I'm with you through all of this. I promise you that," he told me.

Hearing his words made me soften up. This was a hard time for me but being with him always made me feel better, at least for the moment. We just lay there quiet for a few minutes. His chest felt so good against me that I started rubbing on it. Stirring him up, he kissed me passionately. We were just about to start undressing each other when we heard his doorbell ringing out of control. On instinct, we stopped kissing and he jumped up.

"Damn, who the fuck could that be?" Monty asked. "Bruh has a house key of course."

"Go see because it may be an emergency how they're knocking and ringing the doorbell," I told him.

"You're right," he said and headed to answer the door. Not knowing whether or not I should follow him, I sat back on the bed and checked my phone for messages or missed calls.

"Who is it?" I could hear him answer loudly.

"Shonda!" someone screamed. Crazy thoughts went through my head until he opened the door and I heard Monty say, "Damn sis! Why are you knocking like someone is dead?"

"I'm knocking because I saw your car and you needed to answer this damn door," Shonda said with an attitude.

"Look," Monty said. "I've been through a lot the last couple of days. I don't need you coming at me with the foolishness."

"I ain't coming at you with foolishness!" she loudly told him. It was starting to seem evident that his sister was just naturally loud and ghetto as hell. She continued, "How you been in a fire and ain't even call and told me no details? Damn, I'm your sister! And you need to check on Missy. She's missing you and she needs help with your kids!"

"She's going to get help," Monty told her. "She's been acting dumb, so I haven't been calling her but I was going to call her today. Shonda tell her that I want to start getting the kids on weekends. I miss my babies."

"I can tell her," Shonda said. "But, maybe you need to tell her. You need to go talk to her and see your kids. Y'all can discuss the weekend thing then. She loves you and she misses you."

"I'm good," Monty told Shonda. "I'll call her though because we need to discuss the kids. She doesn't need to miss me because we're done!"

"All those years and you can't go see bout her! That's crazy!" Shonda said. "That bitch you been cheating on her with must got some good pussy. Ain't she married? You need to let that hoe go and go back home. You were in the house with her and it caught fire and shit. Fucking with that hoe could have gotten you killed!"

Hearing his sister call me names made me cringe. I wanted to go out there and beat the hell out of her but I decided to stay in my place. There was a part of me that felt bad for

Missy. After all, she was Tasha's friend at one time. I never liked her ass. Before I could get more upset, I heard Monty's voice.

"Look Shonda, this is why I don't fuck with your ass like that now. You're out of line! Stay the fuck out of my business and don't disrespect my girl again!"

"You're always taking up for hoes. Go see your damn kids. Missy been there for you through all the bullshit and cheating! She stayed after you put your hand on her and all! You're wrong Monty! I'm not taking sides. I'm just being real," Shonda said.

Hearing this information made me see red flags. Had he physically put his hands-on Missy before? Was he a big cheater? So many thoughts went through my head.

"Get out!" Monty yelled at Missy. "You take her side over mine. You don't know half the shit she put me through!"

"I'm not taking sides," Shonda said. "She's like my sister. You were with her so long and I just feel bad. She's drinking more. Her mom is getting YOUR kids all the time. All I'm saying is have some sympathy and help out more."

Monty was quiet. "Ok," he told his sister. "Now leave."

"Whatever!" she told him. "I love you but I love her and my niece and nephew too. I'm just trying to make peace."

"You can't make me be with someone that I don't want to be with. And you need to act more like MY sister than hers. Now leave please!" he told her. Without saying another word, I heard the door slam which indicated his sister left.

When he walked in the room, I looked up at him. It was hard to hide the surprise on my face.

"My sister is loud and don't care what she says," Monty said as soon as he walked in the room. "Don't pay her any attention."

I was quiet.

"Baby? You ok?" Monty asked me.

"Yes. It's just so much going on. I shouldn't be here. I'm going to go. It'll be time to pick up my kids soon anyway," I told him.

"Don't go," he told me. "Let's talk. Please don't believe everything my sister said. Missy and I have been through a lot and that is why we don't need to be together."

97

"We'll talk later," I told him as I stood up. "It's not just your sister. It's everything. So much is going on. I need to get my life together. You need to talk to Missy and get your kids. We need space Monty."

"No baby," he told me and stood up too. "Baby, I fell in love with you. Our situations are hard but we can get through them together. We just have to deal with things one day at a time and not give up on each other."

Hearing him say that he loved me made my heart flutter but my mind told me to run. I really needed space just to think. "Baby, I just need some space. I just need a few days to spend time with my family and my babies. I love you too but we're moving too fast. I'm feeling so overwhelmed and stressed. Please just give me a couple of days. That way, you can handle your business with Missy too."

The look on his face told me that he didn't agree but he softened up and said, "Ok baby. I'll give you space."

"Thanks baby," I told him. "I'll call you in a few days."

He nodded his head and we hugged. I didn't let him walk me to the car. When I got in my car and drove off, I let out a sigh. My life was falling apart and it was time that I stopped thinking with my heart and picked up the pieces.

CHAPTER 20

SANDY

It had been a couple of days since the disgusting incident of paying off Lee's kidnapper and having to suck his dick. I'd never felt lower in my life than at that moment. When I got home that day, I immediately showered and brushed my teeth. Lee kept apologizing but I didn't want to hear it. Lea came home later and was happy to see her dad. I told her that I was sick and went to my room and have been in here ever since. Lea was in school now and I finally decided to get up out of the bed. She deserved her mother so I had to get myself together. Tasha had been calling and texting but I told her that I was really sick. There was no way that I was going to tell her everything that went on with me and Lee. Enough was going on in her life as it was.

Lee was now gone. He would be back with Lea later on this afternoon. He'd been so upset about what happened to me because of him. Every night he told me that he was going to see exactly who the big connect was and make his ass pay. I'd told him not to do anything to get in trouble and his life was worth more than that money. Though I said that, part of me wondered if I was a damn fool for doing what I did. After all, this was the man who filmed us having sex and ruined my relationship with Darrin. The blowjob was humiliating and rough. It would take me a while to get the guy's nasty dick taste out of my mouth. Lea had been in to kiss my cheek a few times but we told her we didn't want her to get sick by hanging out in Mommy's room.

I got up and cleaned my house. Lee had been keeping things in order so there wasn't much to do. When I was done, I soaked in hot bubbles in my tub. My mind went into a thousand places. Revenge swirled through my head. Thoughts of how stupid I was for being there for Lee also crossed my mind. Thinking about how caring and helpful he was these last couple of days made my thoughts soften up. The truth was that I still loved Lee. I'd always loved him and probably always will. It was the reason why it was so easy for me to have sex with him when I was with someone else. He'd gone from being a loser to almost the man that I always wanted him to be. He'd worked hard, though illegally, to get his money up and he was very generous with me. That showed me that he cared. Lisa was the reason that he was broke now. That bitch was the person who needed to pay even more than the head of the organization.

My thoughts were interrupted when I heard the front door open. I knew it was Lee with my baby, Lea. For the first time in days, I was excited to see her. There was no way that I'd let a situation get me that down that I don't want to spend time with my baby. After drying off and throwing on a comfortable dress, I walked out of my bedroom.

"Mommy!" Lea said excitedly when she saw me. I gave her a hug.

"Hey baby. How was your day?" I asked her.

"It was fun. Daddy bought us chicken!" she said excitedly.

Holding her hand and walking into the kitchen, I saw that Lee had Popeye's on the table.

"Hey bae," he told me. "Looks like you're feeling better."

"I am," I told him, smiling. For some reason, I felt good. Maybe it was Lea's excitement of being with her daddy and mommy.

He looked at me like he was puzzled. "Well, that's good. Let's eat."

~

Later that night, we tucked Lea in bed. After she was sleep, Lee and I sat in the den. I'd had enough of my room. "Wanna smoke?" he asked me as he pulled out some weed and a blunt.

"Sure," I said. Lee rolled up the weed and lit up the joint. We puffed a few times before he said, "Sandy, I love you. I'm so sorry for everything. Not just the awful things that happened to you recently but everything. For years, you've held me down and I've been ungrateful and resentful. I was so wrong. Please forgive me for everything."

Looking at him I said, "I told you before that I forgive you. I meant it."

Lee smiled and stared at me. "You're so damn beautiful. How could I have been such a damn fool? Sandy, please give me another chance. Let's try it again. I miss being with Lea everyday. I love you and I need you. After giving up the money and saving me the way you did, I know you love me too baby."

Knowing that I should probably run for the hills, I turned to him. "I want to try it too. I love you Lee. Lea loves you. I like us being a family. Please don't make me be a fool for giving us another try."

"I won't," he promised me. "You're the best thing that has ever happened to me. I'll never take that for granted again."

Feeling emotional, we kissed. It had been a while since we'd kissed so passionately. Finally coming up for breath, he moved from my lips to my chest. He gently kissed my chest and pulled my breasts from out of the dress opening. He tickled my nipples with his tongue. It felt so good and I could feel my vagina getting wet. Lee stuck his finger in my wet vagina as he licked my nipples. Moans escaped my lips. Wanting to please me even more, he took his finger and pulled off my panties. Lifting my dress, he began to lick my pussy. As he licked my pussy, I squirmed and moaned. His loving was feeling so good. When I couldn't take it anymore, I reached and touched his head. "Baby, you driving me wild," I let him know. "Gimme some dick baby."

Lee came up from my pussy and kissed me on my lips. Wanting to taste my juices, I tongue kissed him passionately. I stopped kissing him so that he could take his pants and boxers off. When I saw his big dick standing at attention, I opened my legs wide. He slowly eased his dick into my pussy.

"Damn baby!" he said when he felt how wet and warm my pussy was. He slowly stuck his dick further in my pussy. We made love in the den from the sofa to the floor. Even through everything, I realized that I loved this man from the bottom of my heart. Tonight, our lovemaking was so good and we fell in love all over again.

CHAPTER 21

TASHA

The kids stood around the den as I checked to make sure they were properly dressed and ready for school. Mom had decided to stay in her own house. She needed time to herself and I understood completely. All the kids in this house could run anyone crazy. There were Nitra's two kids, my three kids and now Tyvonna. She'd been staying with us the past couple of days since Ty picked her up from school the other day. Latisha still hadn't contacted him and her cousin hadn't heard from her. She always seemed like the type of bitch who didn't have time for her kids. Ty was happy about spending extra time with Tyvonna so it worked out good.

Nitra helped out with the kids a lot. She'd found an apartment that would be ready to move in next week. Part of me was going to miss her help. I'd have to ask Mom to help out with the baby some days so I can do some work. She needed the distraction, in my opinion. Nitra had gone to sign the lease to her apartment and answer a few more questions about the fire to the detective. Ty was getting dressed because he was dropping the kids off to school. Baby TJ and I would be here. Sandy was finally feeling better and she was going to stop by after she dropped Lea off to school.

Ty came in to grab a bite. "Hey baby," he said and kissed me on the lips. "Y'all kids about ready? We're leaving in a few."

"Yes, we're ready daddy," Tyvonna said. She seemed happy to be with her daddy and around the kids. The other kids started talking and giggling. Within a few minutes, I was kissing them all goodbye as they left for the day. TJ lay in the playpen sleep. He'd just went back to sleep after waking me up early this morning. There was so much going on; I hadn't started planning my wedding. It was the end of the week so next week I would start working on some things.

The doorbell rang and I let Sandy in. "Hey girl!" I said giving her a hug. I hadn't seen her or talked to her much in days and I missed my friend.

"Hey," she said. She walked in and peeped at TJ sleeping.

"Let's talk in the kitchen," I said. "We'll hear if he wakes up." We walked over to the kitchen. "Want some coffee? Want me to fix you breakfast? Kids ate oatmeal before school but I can whip up some grits and eggs or something for us."

"Actually, I am hungry," Sandy said. "I haven't eaten much these past few days. I'm better now though. How is your Mom doing after everything?"

"Girl! She's home. She wants time to herself. Her ass went to Aunt Kathy's house and had us fighting!"

"What?" Sandy laughed. "What happened?"

I gave Sandy the details about the fight. She laughed her ass off.

"That ain't it!" I told her. "How about I caught Nitra and Monty fucking?"

"No!" Sandy said. "Damn, I missed a lot!"

"Yes, you did and I'm not finished bitch. There's more! Tyvonna is with us now because Latisha's trifling ass has been missing in action the last couple of days. She left the kids with her cousin so Ty got Tyvonna."

"Damn!" Sandy said. "So much happened in just a few days!"

"Yes!" I said. "How am I going to have time to plan my wedding now with so much going on?"

"You'll have time," she told me. "I'll help you."

"Thank you," I told her. "Man, I missed you. You should have let me take care of you when you were sick."

"No, you had so much going on," she said. "Besides, Lee was there to help out."

Thinking I must have been hearing things, I asked her, "Did you say Lee was there to help out? With all that went on with y'all? Why was he around?"

Sandy looked uncomfortable before she said, "He wanted to see Lea and I needed help with her. He apologized about everything and it was sincere."

Shaking my head, I said, "Really? You really think his apology was sincere or did he need that money he was trying to get from you a while ago?"

She looked offended and I immediately regretted my words. "I'm sorry sis," I told her, softening my tone. "That was out of line. I'm just on edge with everything that's been happening. Mom is heart broken. Nitra is going through bullshit. I just want to protect you."

Standing up she said, "I understand. I know you love me. But, I got to go."

"Where are you going? Breakfast will be done soon," I reasoned with her. Why did I have to say what I said? But shit, I was just being honest. "Sorry if I offended you. Don't leave please."

"Lee and I are back together," she blurted out to me. There was definitely shock on my face. It seemed like this had happened overnight. He was the reason that she lost a good man. The man filmed them having sex.

Not knowing what to say to her announcement, I remained quiet. She didn't say anything either. Finally, I spoke. "If it makes you happy, then do what you choose. I just want you to be happy and please don't give him the money that he was asking about." As soon as I said that last sentence, Sandy's face changed. Why'd I have to have such a big mouth?

CHAPTER 22

SANDY

Highly offended by Tasha's comment, I got up and grabbed my purse. "I'll talk to you later Tasha."

"Don't leave," Tasha told me. "Breakfast is almost done. I'm sorry that I offended you. I'm just concerned."

"You don't need to be concerned about me," I let her know. "You have enough going on in your life, so don't worry about mine." She always acts like her damn shit don't stink, I thought to myself. Maybe I was mad at myself because I did give him the money and was too embarrassed to tell her what happened with that.

"You're right," she told me. I knew that she loved me but that didn't mean that she ran my life. Shit, if it wasn't for Ty she would've probably gone back to Terry's sorry ass by now.

"I'm going to leave though," I told her. "There are some errands that I have to run. I'll call you later."

Tasha looked sad when she said, "Ok. I wish you could have stayed for breakfast. Sandy, I'm so sorry if I offended you.

You're like my sister and I love you. I just want to protect you. I wasn't trying to make you feel any type of way about being back with Lee. If you're happy, I promise that I'm happy for you." It was evident that she was sincere and her concern was out of love.

"I'll call you later," I told her and then hugged her.

Opening the door to leave, Nitra was pulling up in her car. As I walked to my car, we passed each other.

"Hey Sandy," she told me. "Glad you're feeling better. Where are you going?"

Hugging her I said, "You're looking good. I'm glad you're ok."

"Thanks," she told me.

"Well, I'll see y'all later," I said and got in my car and pulled off. Lee was gone handling some business, so I planned on going home and chilling. Tasha could be so offensive. After everything I'd been through, I didn't need the bullshit from my friend. Driving home, I thought of ways to find Lisa's ass. A private detective probably could help. Dealing with a street-smart bitch like Lisa, I'd have to find a street smart private detective. I needed to find one who could blend in with the streets. That is exactly what I'm going to do! I thought to myself. That bitch would pay!

CHAPTER 23

NITRA

After hugging Sandy goodbye, I walked in the house. Tasha seemed to just be finishing up breakfast. "You're cooking?" I asked her, puzzled. "No kids are here."

"Bitch, I got to eat too," she told me.

Laughing I said, "Well there better be enough for me."

"Yes there is," she told me. "Sandy had to go before I was done."

"I saw her," I said. "Glad she's better. She couldn't stay for breakfast though?"

"I think that I offended her," Tasha told me. "She told me that Lee helped her out when she was sick."

"Oh, and you had a problem with that?" I knew my sister like a book.

"No," Tasha said then snuck in, "I just reminded her of all he's done."

I shook my head. "You know you can't come between dick and pussy."

"They're back together," Tasha said. "It just happened so sudden and I know he needed money for some mess that he had going on. I just was concerned that he may have been using her."

"You got a point but she's grown," I told Tasha. "People have to make their own mistakes and you just have to be a friend and help her if she falls. Don't be judgmental."

"You're right," she told me. "I feel bad. I'll text her another apology later."

"Do that," I said. We sat and ate breakfast. I washed the dishes and cleaned the kitchen while Tasha tended to TJ. She changed him and fed him. My nephew was so cute. After cleaning, I went to my room to lie down. My night had been sleepless. Monty had been giving me space but last night he sent a text saying he missed me. Part of me really missed him too but I didn't respond.

Lying in my bed, I stared at the ceiling. The detective had asked me more questions about whether or not I had enemies. There were no enemies that I knew of. He questioned me about my relationship with Kevin and our custody battle. He let me know that their investigation was in full swing and they would let me know what they found out.

I didn't know when I fell asleep but I woke up to my phone ringing back to back.

Looking at the time, I'd been sleep a few hours. The phone had stopped ringing but I knew it would ring again. It was Monty. There were 4 missed calls from him. As I predicted, the phone rang again and I answered.

"Hello," I answered sounding slightly groggy.

"Hey baby. You ok? You weren't answering," Monty said.

"Yes, I'm ok. I was sleep," I told him.

"Would you like to do lunch? I know you'll be getting the kids in a few," he told me.

Feeling bad for not talking to him for a few days, I agreed. Monty was good to me but I was feeling smothered. Kevin could use me dating Monty against me in court. Though I like him and wanted to see where our relationship went, I wanted to slow down for a while. Everything was beginning to be just too much. I didn't know what to do with my life.

After getting myself together, I met Monty at the agreed upon restaurant. He was there when I arrived. He was looking good with his jeans and polo shirt on.

"Hey baby," he said and we hugged and kissed quickly on the lips. "How have you been?"

"As well as could be," I told him. "So much to do and so many thoughts are going through my head."

"I understand," he told me. "You know you can call me anytime that you want to talk or vent. My shoulder is here for you."

"I know," I told him. "I just wanted to take some time to myself to think and be there for my kids. First, Kevin moved out. Now, we have to stay somewhere else for a while. Getting them comfortable and adjusted to our new life needs to be my first priority right now."

"You're right baby," Monty said. "Missy finally agreed to let me see the kids. At first, she didn't answer any of my calls and texts but she texted me earlier and said that I can come when they get out of school. Hopefully, we can discuss me getting them some weekends."

"That'll be great," I said.

We ate and chatted for a while. Our conversation was good and it made me miss being around him. When we left, he walked me to my car.

"I'll call you after I see my kids," he told me. "Or do you prefer me wait until tomorrow?"

"Call me so you can tell me how things went," I told him. Missy was a bitch so she probably would put up a fight. It wasn't right that I was sleeping with her man but their relationship was dead. Guilt did set in from time to time. Kevin didn't deserve me cheating though he could have worked more on the relationship a long time ago.

"Ok, I will," he said. He kissed me passionately and then I got in the car. Damn, that kiss had my pussy soaking wet. Monty was charming and there was something about his swag that I loved. We had an attraction that wouldn't let me stay away no matter how much I tried. On the way to the school, I wondered if I was being too hard on him for saying that I needed space. We both handled our significant others wrong but that didn't mean we couldn't be together one day.

CHAPTER 24

MISSY

I sat on the porch and waited on the school bus to drop the kids off. Not feeling like cooking, I'd ordered Chinese food delivery. I didn't feel like leaving the house. Knowing that I needed to get my life on track, I'd done some thinking today. Unfortunately, my thinking was partnered with some drinking. Monty called to say that he wanted to see the kids and I told him that he could come. After everything that he did to me, I still loved his ass.

The bus dropped the kids off and they ran up to the porch. Fortunately for me, I had good kids. They knew mama was going through some things and they were so helpful and understanding. My daughter helped me with cleaning the house and cooking. "Hey mama," my daughter said and she hugged me. My baby was in the 5th grade. She was getting so big.

"Hey baby," I said and hugged her back. "Hey son," I told my son as he followed behind on the porch. He was in 3rd grade and he looked just like Monty.

"Hey mom," he said. Something seemed sad in his voice.

"What's wrong baby?" I asked him.

"He was fighting in school," my daughter told me. "His teacher told me to give you this." She handed me an envelope. Opening the envelope, I read where the teacher said that Lil Monty had punched some little boy. She said Lil Monty was the aggressor.

"Monty, you were fighting?" I asked him. He just looked at me sadly. "I asked you a question."

He started nodding his head yes.

"Why?" I asked him. Before he could answer, Monty's car pulled up in the driveway. When the kids saw him getting out of the car, they ran off the porch and met him to the bottom of the steps.

"Daddy!" Lil Monty screamed as he and his sister gave Monty a hug.

"Hey babies!" he said while hugging them.

Walking on the porch and holding both kids' hands, Monty said to me, "Hey. How have you been?"

"Ok," I told him. My heart started hurting when he talked to me for some reason. "Lil Monty was fighting in school today. Maybe you can talk to him about it?"

"Definitely," he said then looked at Lil Monty. Our son put his head down in shame. He knew fighting was wrong. "Can I take them out to eat and bring them back in a few hours? I'll talk to them and then we can have a conversation."

"Ok," I told him. Going into the house, I fixed myself some of the Chinese food that I'd ordered. Feeling lonely, I poured myself some gin and juice. Being sober made me think about the awful things that I did in the past couple of weeks. It wasn't me. I was hurt and scorn and had turned into a whole different person. The guilt of it all ate me up every night. After eating, I sat on the couch and drink. When Monty brought the kids home, we needed to talk.

A couple of hours went by and I heard Monty's car pull up in the driveway. Standing up, I opened the door so that they wouldn't have to knock. Monty and the kids walked in.

"How was dinner?" I asked the kids.

"It was good," my daughter said as she walked in. "Daddy, are you going to stay and tuck us in?"

Monty looked like he didn't know how to respond then he said, "Sure. You both go take your baths and get your pajamas on. When you're done, I'll tuck you in."

"Ok," my daughter said and headed towards the bathroom.

"Can you give me a bath?" our son asked Monty. It was obvious that he didn't want to leave his daddy's side.

"Ok I will after your sister's done," he told him. Monty sat on the couch with Lil Monty. "Do you have homework?" he asked Lil Monty. Lil Monty shook his head no.

"Are you sure?" I asked him. "Your grades are dropping." He still shook his head no.

"His grades are dropping?" Monty asked me.

Anger filled me because of the way he asked me. It was like in an accusatory tone. "Yes, his grades are dropping," I said with attitude. "And he's misbehaving as you can see from him fighting today. But don't look at me like it's my fault. You're the one walked out on your damn kids." The gin had me feeling angry.

"Did I say it was your fault?" Monty asked me. Looking at Monty he said, "Son, go in your room and find your pajamas. I'll come get you for your bath soon." Lil Monty nodded his head sadly and then walked to his room. Turning back to me Monty said, "There are some things that shouldn't be said in front of the kids. And I wasn't accusing your ass. That's just your guilt."

"Guilt?" I asked. "What guilt? You're the guilty one who wants to lay up with a bitch instead of being here for your kids. It's hard on them since you're not here."

"That's why I came today," Monty said. "I miss my babies. All you and I did was argue and that's what we're still doing. That's why I stopped calling you. Our arguing wears me out. Can I start getting them on weekends? I miss them and I want to give you a break sometimes."

"And take them where?" I asked him. The alcohol was really kicking in. "You're not taking them to that bitch Nitra's house!"

Monty shook his head. "You know I'm staying with my brother. That's where we'll be. But, I have the right to take my kids where I want. Don't start the shit Missy. We're over and you have to start dealing with that. Sober up and get your self together."

Highly offended, I screamed "Sober up! Nigga you sober up! You're acting like you ain't handle me and your kids fucked up! You were fucking my friend's sister! That's wrong! And you act like I'm supposed to be cool with that shit!"

He was quiet then he said, "Missy, I'm sorry. I'll always love you. We just weren't right for each other. We were on different paths."

"Fuck that," I said. By now tears were pouring down my eyes. "All these years that I put up with your shit and this is how you treat me? I didn't always club or drink. Remember when I made sure you came home to cooked meals? Remember the different hoes you used to cheat on me with? I still stayed with you! When I tried to leave, you begged me to stay! You ruined my fucking life and you think you can just walk out and be happy with some bitch?" Anger seeped inside of me and I began punching him. He tried holding my arms but couldn't. I punched him in the eye and in the face several times. Finally, he was able to grab hold of both of my arms.

"Cut this shit out!" he told me. "This is why I don't want your ass!"

Crying, I lost control again. "Nigga, how many times have you put your hands on me? Made me have sex when I didn't want to? Don't act like I'm the fucking bad guy!" I was punching him again as I said this. The hits must have been hurting him because he shoved me back real hard and I flew into the sofa.

He looked angry as he came towards me on the sofa and started punching me. The truth must have hit a nerve. Punching him back, we fought like two people in the street. His hits were hurting me. I used my nails to scratch and hit him with all my might. Trying to protect myself, I picked up the lamp and it hit his back and arm. The kids came in the room screaming and hollering in tears!

"Stop fighting! Stop fighting!" Lil Monty screamed. Our daughter, Montasia, was crying to. She had the phone in her hand. I wondered if she'd called the police on us.

"It's ok," I told them. "Go in the room and lie down. Daddy's leaving." Just as I said that, there was a loud knock at the door. Scared it was the police, I didn't move. Then I heard someone say, "Open the door! It's me Shonda!"

Feeling relieved, I opened the door to let her in.

"What the hell?" she said looking at me and Monty. I could taste blood coming from my lip and I saw blood on his arm and neck. We must have looked tore down. Monty walked past her without acknowledging her and left. She just shook her head at him. Before she can think to scold me, I burst out crying. Knowing I needed it, she walked over and gave me a hug. My life was falling apart and I didn't know what to do.

CHAPTER 25

TASHA

Ty and I were cuddled on our bed in the room. The kids were in their bed finally. TJ was asleep in his room right across from ours. The baby monitor was on the dresser so that we could hear him. Since it was Friday, we had movie night with them after school. Earlier that day, Nitra moved into her new apartment. She'd just gotten the key and only had an air mattress in her room. She was getting furniture delivered in the morning and wanted to sleep there so she would be there already when they came. Mom kept her kids tonight and planned to bring them to her tomorrow after their beds were set up. Mom had still been isolated in her house the past few days but she did call to check in at least once a day. She assured me that she was fine. Her grandbabies should be good company for her tonight. I didn't send my kids with them because that would be too many on her right now.

We were watching a movie and finally happy to relax. Interrupting our movie, Ty's cell phone rung. I gave him the side eye as he answered. I hoped that it wasn't work related because he'd been working a lot as it is and these kids were tiring me out alone. We still hadn't heard from Latisha. Her cousin was still caring for her son. Being the nice guy that he was, Ty helped out the cousin with the child by buying clothes and giving the cousin money to help out with groceries and things. I didn't mind because he was Tyvonna's brother and the cousin was nice to keep him knowing she had kids of her own to take care of too.

"Hello?" Ty answered. "What? I don't think it's that serious. She's probably laid up with some dude. Well ok. It's up to you since she's your family. Keep me informed. Thanks."

Ty turned on the lamp on the side of the bed. "Latisha's cousin said she's filing a missing persons report. She seems to think it's been too long and Latisha's never been missing in action more than a couple of days."

"The fact that she's been missing in action before says enough," I said.

"True. She sounded really worried though. I told her that I didn't think it was necessary but she's her family and she knows her better than me," he said.

"I guess you're right," I said. "I hope she's ok for her kids' sake."

"Yea me too. I think she's ok though," he said. "She probably wanted a break or maybe she ran into some sucker with money."

"You're a mess," I told him and laughed.

"I love you baby," he told me. "And thanks for accepting Tyvonna into our house."

"Of course," I said. "I love her like she's my own. Kids are innocent. Teriana loves having a sister around."

"Yes, they're getting very close and I like that," he said coming back on the bed, he kissed me. We kissed passionately as I lay back on the bed. When we came up for air, we helped each other strip naked. Ty began sucking on my neck then my breasts. He sucked one nipple at a time. My pussy juices spilled because it felt so good.

"Fuck me baby," I told him. "You see how wet you got this pussy?" He touched my pussy to feel the wetness.

"Damn baby," he said and then he started licking between my legs. Just when I didn't think I could get wetter, I did. He seemed hungry as he licked and slurped on my pussy.

I started moaning uncontrollably until I said, "I can't take it baby. I need to feel your dick."

Ty flipped me over on my stomach and stuck his dick slowly in my pussy from the back. I had my head down on the bed and my ass in the air as he fucked me like I requested. "Is this what you wanted baby?" Ty said as he pumped his dick into my pussy. Panting I said, "Yes baby. Yes baby." It was feeling so good that I could barely talk. After a while, we both couldn't take it anymore and he came in my pussy at the same time that I came. He sprawled out next to me on the bed.

"I love you woman," he told me.

"I love you too," I told him. We caught our breaths and I fell asleep on his chest.

~

The next morning, I was awakened by TJ's cries. Throwing on my robe, I rushed to his nursery. As soon as I picked him up, he stopped crying. I gave him a kiss and he smiled. I changed his pamper and went to get him a bottle out of the refrigerator. He was getting so chunky. Not only did I always put cereal in his bottle but he also ate oatmeal, grits and other soft foods. He was a greedy baby but keeping him full had him sleeping all night.

When he was done, I burped him. Ty came down and grabbed him. "Baby, you can wash up. I'll get the kids up and fix them cereal."

"Ok," I told him then went upstairs and showered and dressed. When I came back down, the kids were at the kitchen table. They all greeted me and I gave them all a kiss. Ty was sitting down playing with TJ.

"Hey baby," he told me. I love this man, I thought to myself. Before I could respond, the doorbell rang and I went to answer the door thinking that it was Nitra. Who else would come over without calling? Imagine my shock when I saw Latisha's cousin with a police officer standing next to her.

"May I help you?" I asked them. The cousin had tears in her eyes like she'd been crying.

"We need to speak with Tyvon Jenkins," he told me.

"May I ask what this is about?" I asked.

"Ma'am, we need to talk to him," the officer told me.

"Ok," I said then shut the door and went to the kitchen. "Baby, come to the door," I told him. I didn't want to say who was there in front of the kids. He got up with TJ in his hand. When he left the kitchen I whispered, "Baby, the police are at the door. Put TJ in the playpen in here with his toys." Doing as told, Ty put TJ down. At first, he wanted to fuss then he started playing with his little toys. We opened the door and stepped out onto the porch.

"Hey. May I help you?" Ty asked the officer when we got on the porch. Our porch area was circular like a balcony. My flowers and plants decorated it and there were chairs to sit on. There were still some things that I needed to add to decorate it more. TJ kept me so busy and that's why my big house had so many unfinished areas that weren't yet decorated.

"Yes. I have some questions," the officer said. "There was a missing person's report done on a Latisha Anderson. Do you know her?"

"Yes. We have a daughter," he told the officer. Looking at the cousin he asked, "Are you ok Leslie?"

"Don't fucking talk to me," she started crying.

"What's wrong?" Ty asked her. He looked confused. They'd been getting along and he'd been helping her out financially with Latisha's son.

The officer handed her a tissue then he said, "Ma'am. Please refrain from talking. I understand you're hurting but please let me ask the questions. That's why I didn't want you to follow me here. This is a police investigation."

Leslie wiped her eyes and didn't say anything else. "What is going on?" I asked the officer. It was confusing as to why they were here.

"Latisha Anderson was found dead. We'd actually found her body a couple of days ago but didn't know her identity. When Leslie reported her cousin missing, we were able to put it together later by DNA."

"What?" Ty asked. He and I were shocked. I was speechless. His eyes were wide open.

"Yes. The DNA reports show that the body found belonged to Latisha Anderson. We need to ask you some questions. When was the last time you saw her?" the officer asked, looking at Ty. Ty answered that it had been weeks. He answered more questions concerning their relationship and Tyvonna. Leslie mentioned that Ty wasn't Tyvonna's real dad and would do anything for custody.

"He had visitation rights and gave Latisha money. He didn't need to do anything for custody so I don't know what the hell you're trying to say," I angrily told Leslie. I understood her pain but I'd be damned if she was trying to imply that my man harmed her cousin. He had no reason to.

"Whatever, who else would kill my cousin?" she cried. "We only had each other. No other family."

"We understand your pain," Ty said, "But I would never harm her. What will I tell Tyvonna?" Ty looked so hurt and heartbroken. I hugged him tight. "I'm going to have to tell that little girl that her mother died!" Tears filled his eyes.

The police officer just observed quietly. "Well, here's my card," he told Ty after we broke loose from our hug. "Call me if there is any pertinent information that you forgot to mention. We'll be in touch."

"You're just going to let him go?" Leslie asked. "I told you he was the only one with motive to kill my cousin."

"Let's go," the officer told her sternly. He sensed she was going to lose control.

"Oh, I'll be back for Tyvonna," Leslie said as the officer escorted her to her car and watched her drive off. Once she left, he got in his car and pulled off too. Ty and I just stared at each other. We both still were in shock. We didn't move from standing on the porch until we heard TJ crying. How was he going to break the news to Tyvonna that her mother was dead?

CHAPTER 26

SANDY

I pulled up in Tasha's driveway. She'd called me to apologize about everything and I accepted. Part of me knew some of the things she said were right. My focus was elsewhere now. Lee and I were building a life for our daughter. When Tasha told me about Latisha being found dead, my heart dropped. I'd beat the girl up before and called her all kinds of names but never would I want her dead. She was a mother and I felt sorry for her kids. Who could have killed her? How were the kids going to deal with their mother's death?

Tasha opened her front door before I could get out of the car good. She ran and gave me a hug. "I miss you friend," she said.

"I missed you too," I told her while hugging her back.

We walked into her house and Ty and Ms. Karen was sitting in the living room. TJ was in her mom's lap. The other kids must have been in their rooms. Not seeing her since the incident, I went over to hug Ms. Karen.

"How are you doing?" I asked her.

"Good," she told me. It was evident that she was still a little sad.

Sitting down I said, "I can't believe Latisha's dead. That's so sad."

"Yes," Tasha said. "I pray the police find out who did it."

"Me too," I said.

Tasha's doorbell rang. Ty got up to the answer it. A few minutes later, he came back to the den and said, "Ms. Karen. That's Bernard at the door. He is adamant about talking to you. He says he just wants one conversation to explain everything."

Tasha looked mad. Her mom answered, "He's been texting and calling all week. It's getting annoying. I'll speak to him once and that's it. I'm ready to get an annulment and be done with this shit. We do need to talk first though."

Even through hurt, Ms. Karen knew how to make you laugh. I'd always liked being around her ever since I was a teenager. She handed Tasha her child and went out the door to talk to her new husband. Everything was just so crazy. Any person would lose their mind dealing with all of their family issues. I had issues too.

"What the hell his nasty ass want?" Tasha asked looking mad.

Ty laughed at her. "Tasha, they're married. They do need to have a conversation. Closure is needed. Maybe they can work things out."

"I don't know bout that," Tasha said. "He's just nasty."

"Most men are," I burst out laughing. The mood in the room had lightened but I had to ask some dark questions, "So how did they say Latisha died? Where did they find her?"

"She was choked to death," Tasha said. "They also said she was hit in the head with a blunt object. Someone attacked her."

"Damn," I said. "Now I feel bad about everything that happened with her and us."

"Me too," Tasha said. At that moment, Ms. Karen walked in.

"Tasha, I'm about to go," Ms. Karen said. "I'll call you in the morning."

.

"You're going with Bernard?" Tasha asked her mom.

"I'll call you in the morning," her mom told her sternly and left.

Tasha frowned. She always wanted to control everything.

"Leave her alone," I told her. "That's her husband. It's between them if they work it out." She annoyed me with that shit.

"You're right," she told me. "And I'm happy for you if you and Lee are back together."

"Thanks," I told her. She got under my skin sometimes but I loved her. "We are back together and I'm happy."

"Well, I'm happy for you," she told me. She seemed genuine.

Feeling my phone vibrate, I checked my text messages. It was a message from Lee.

Can you meet me now?

I texted him back: *Sure. Where?*

He wanted to meet at a restaurant that was near my house. Looking up from my phone, Tasha was staring at me.

"Well, damn. That must be Lee," she said teasing.

"Yes," I said to her. "I'm going to meet him somewhere. I'll call you tomorrow. We need to do lunch or something."

"Definitely," she told me and we hugged. I left to meet Lee.

CHAPTER 27

NITRA

My place was all set up. It was small but cute. It was temporary so that didn't matter. Mom had brought the kids back and they loved their new beds. Kevin asked to get them for a couple of days and I let him. I still had some unpacking to do so they would be out of my way. He deserved to spend time with them anyway. He just needed to know that I was in charge and I had main custody. If he wanted to play with me about my kids, it would get ugly.

Monty called me and said that he wanted to come over. He'd gone to spend time with his kids so I assumed he wanted to tell me how things went. There was a knock at my door and I looked in the peephole to see it was Monty. Opening the door, I shrieked.

"Damn! What happened to you?" I asked him. He had scratches on his face and there was a big gauze bandage covering part of his arm. His eye even looked bruised. After he came in, I hugged him softly. He was quiet and sat on the couch. As if ashamed, he put his head down.

"Baby, I don't know where Missy and I went so wrong," he said. "She used to be the love of my life. Now she hates me and I can't stand being around her."

"What? What happened?" I asked him. We sat on the couch. "You're banged up!"

"I went to see the kids. I took them to dinner. Lil Monty wanted me to give him a bath. Trying to be cordial with Missy turned into us fighting. She hit me with a lamp and all," he told me.

"Damn! So, did you call the police? She fucked you up!" I told him. He couldn't let her get away with battering him. He looked a mess!

Shaking his head, he said, "No. She makes me so angry and left me no choice but to defend myself and hit her back. Calling the police would have gotten me in trouble too. She has a few bruises as well."

"What?" I asked him, perplexed. "You bruised her up? So, you guys were all out trying to kill each other?" Many thoughts raced through my head. Was I dealing with a woman beater? "Why didn't you just leave instead of letting it get so bad?"

"I couldn't!" he said. "She kept fighting me. My daughter called my sister and I was able to leave once she came. It killed me to see my kids crying. Missy just refused to be cordial. It's like she's lost her damn mind. I don't know who she is anymore. I know that I hurt her but our relationship had been in trouble a long time before I fell for you." He sighed.

For some reason, I felt sorry for him. My own life was hectic right now and I had my own custody issues. There was a part of me telling me to run from this man. But, there was also a part of me that felt that I was falling in love with him and we were the cause of each other's problems so we should stick it out together.

"Baby, let me help clean and bandage you up the proper way. I could tell you did this shit yourself," I laughed to lighten the mood. He smiled too. I cleaned him up and we lay in bed and cuddled all night. We didn't say much. We just held each other until we fell asleep. I'm sure he was feeling pain from his fight with Missy. There were consequences to our affair and we were both feeling them.

CHAPTER 28

KAREN (TASHA & NITRA'S MOM)

Bernard had been calling me everyday but I'd been ignoring him. He hadn't tried to come by my house but my locks were changed any way. When he came to Tasha's, I felt it was time to talk. I couldn't have his ass showing up to my daughter's house. In all the years of my life, many men came and went. That was how I liked it. I used them for what I needed. There was no love. They paid my bills and we had a good time. That was all I ever needed from a man. My girls grew up and moved out, so I moved out of town. It didn't work out with the guy that I moved out of town with but I met Bernard later down the line. He convinced me that we needed to move closer to my daughters. He was the first man who seemed to truly care. Like a fool, I fell in love and married him. For him to do the unthinkable and mess with my sister hurt my heart. My sister was always a jealous whore. She'd fucked guys behind me before but it was a long time ago. I'd done the same to her in earlier years. But, I thought that I could trust Bernard.

When we left Tasha's house, Bernard and I went to my home to talk. He started crying and explained some shocking things to me. He confessed that he was head of a big drug organization. He was semi-retired, so all he did was collect money and everyone else did the dirty work. He put his sons in charge but he came around to check on the money. I knew he had sons but I thought they were estranged. He'd made it seem like they didn't have a good relationship. Turns out, he just didn't want me to meet them. My sister Kathy found out what he did because she used cocaine. They bumped into each other when he was collecting money from one of his sons at a drug house. She was leaving the house when she saw him. She'd done drugs in the past but I thought she was off of it. Because he didn't want me to find out what he really did and why he really wanted me to move back to this city, he gave her free drugs all the time. Cocaine explained why she would betray me. At my wedding party that Tasha threw for me, my sister Kathy was high and acting jealous and belligerent. She told Bernard that he picked the wrong sister and grabbed his dick. She promised that she would tell everyone there that he sold drugs if he kept resisting her so he let her suck his dick. That's when I caught them.

Of course, I didn't believe anything that he was saying at first. But, he seemed sincere when he cried and begged me to believe him and give him another chance. There was no real excuse for him letting my sister suck his dick. She put him on the spot but he also was a man and I know that his ass was curious. It wasn't smart of me but I decided to give him another chance. Bernard had money that could take care of me for life and I wanted it. I really loved him but I also loved money too. For how he treated me, he gave me a large sum of cash and bought me many gifts. I planned on keeping the cash saved and letting him continue to spend his money.

Tasha and Nitra wouldn't understand the truth so I decided to tell them part of the story. I would tell them just the part about their aunt being back on cocaine and forcing herself on him. They would surely think that I was dumb to take him back but I didn't care. Shit, I was set for life financially. Nitra was dumb for cheating and breaking up her marriage. Tasha went through some stuff last year that was on her fault. We all were guilty of being a little dumb over men. I was too old to care about what people thought.

Bernard promised that he would stop dealing with the business all around and let his sons take over. He also agreed to let me meet his sons soon.

CHAPTER 29

TASHA

It was the day of Latisha's funeral and Ty and I were there with Tyvonna. It was so hard seeing Tyvonna's hurt after learning that her mother was dead. She'd been so sad. Though Leslie still had an attitude, she wasn't accusing Ty anymore. Besides, she needed our help with the funeral expenses. Mom kept TJ so that we didn't have to bring him with us. Terry and Teriana were with their dad for the weekend. We wanted to be able to give our full attention to Tyvonna.

Missy attended the funeral since she and Latisha had become good friends. Leslie let Missy sit in the front row along with us because they didn't have much family. There were just a few older cousins. Missy didn't speak to me. I guess she was mad that Nitra and Monty were together. It wasn't my fault. Tyvonna cried during the funeral. My heart broke for that little girl. Ty and I was all she had now. I planned on loving her like she was my very own daughter. My hands would be full but I would be ok.

After the funeral, we stopped by Leslie's house to eat. We didn't plan on staying long but we wanted Tyvonna to see her family and tell them goodbye. Once we were in the house, I noticed that Missy had scratches on her face. Her dumb ass must have been fighting someone.

"What are you staring at?" she asked me. I must have been staring too long.

"Oh nothing," I said. I didn't want there to be trouble on this sad day.

She eyed me up and down. "It better not had been nothing bitch," she had the nerve to say.

Looking at the red cup in her hand, I knew that she was drinking alcohol. The juice was giving her courage. She could have been just grieving her friend. After all, she didn't seem to have any other friends. Ty looked at me as if to tell me to keep my cool. The look in my eyes let him know that I was ready to go. We left from where the bitch Missy was standing and went to mingle with a few other guests. Not long after, we left and took Tyvonna home. It was because of Tyvonna that I kept my cool.

CHAPTER 30

SANDY

Lea was sleep and I was in the living room when Lee walked in the door. "Hey baby," he told me.

"Hey," I responded and stood up as he hugged and kissed me. Even though hideous things had happened, Lee and I had gotten so much closer. He'd swallowed his pride when it came to me. There was nothing we didn't talk about and I loved it because communication was everything. Losing good communication was why we were disconnected emotionally for so many years. I was falling back in love with him.

He sat next to me and said, "Bae, things are going so well with us. I've even found a job that is going to start in a couple of weeks. If I can just find that bastard responsible for hurting you, we can pay him back and move on with our lives."

"Maybe we should just move on with our lives without finding him. Let's just let it go and be happy." I told him.

"I've got a lead on a spot that the guy goes to. He goes there to collect money from the heads of the organization. I'm thinking about checking it out."

Feeling worried I said, "Baby let's just let it go and move on with our lives. You're going to start a job and I still have a savings. We'll be good."

"I'll handle it from here," he told me. "You stay out of it. I won't be good until I pay that fucker back for what he did to you. You just take care of Lea."

"Ok baby," I told him and we kissed. Part of me didn't want to stay away and let him handle it. I'd lost a lot in this situation too.

Lee stood up and scooped me up off of the sofa. "Boy!" I shrieked. "Put me down! You bet not drop me!" I couldn't help but laugh at his crazy ass. Lee was definitely different and more spontaneous these days. He carried me to the bedroom. When we arrived, he dropped me down on the bed. Hovering over me, he took off my clothes.

"Damn baby! You're so beautiful," he told me. "I love you so much. It's as if I actually see the person you really are. That person is sweet, smart, beautiful, and tough."

Naked and blushing I said, "Thank you baby. I see the person that you really are too. You're a good man. You're protective and loving. I love you too baby."

Lee started rubbing my feet. Then, he started sucking on my toes. He knew that would turn me on. When he was done, he stripped naked. He sucked on my breasts and I got so horny. It wasn't long before I grabbed his big, hard dick and inserted it into my pussy. His dick was the missing piece of my puzzle. It felt so good. It was like when we first fell in love many years ago. We spent the rest of the night making love.

CHAPTER 31

NITRA

Monty and I were awakened by my phone ringing. Sleepily, I looked at the caller ID and saw that it was Kevin calling.

"Hello?" I answered.

"What are you doing? I've been calling for an hour!" he yelled into the phone. I was really getting sick of his shit.

"Look, we're not together anymore. I don't answer to you and I don't have to answer my damn phone for you! Now, is my babies ok?" I asked him with much attitude.

"Yes, they are. And it's a good thing because you wouldn't be available," he told me. "I'm on my way to bring you the kids. The police want to talk to me about that house fire and I don't want the kids with me when I go to the station."

"Good! Bring me my babies," I told him and hung up. Wondering what the police wanted to talk to Kevin about, I got up out of the bed. Looking at Monty I said, "Baby, you got to go.

Kevin is bringing the kids back because he has to go to the police station. I don't want him or them to see you here."

Monty slowly got up. "Are we going to eventually tell the kids about us? Are we going to be together? It seems weird to run when your ex comes around."

"It's not about my ex," I told him. "It's more about the kids. Their parents split and their house caught fire. They're going through so much. We have to treat the situation sensitively."

"I understand," Monty said as he finished getting dressed. His face didn't read that he understood though. While walking him to the door, we heard a knock.

"Damn, he must have been already in route. You can just chill in the room until I get the kids together then you can sneak out later."

"Cool," he said and went back to the bedroom. After more knocking, I opened the door. My babies rushed in and gave me a hug.

"Hey sweethearts," I told them and hugged them.

"Bout time you answered the door," Kevin said. I just shook my head. He was a real asshole. He continued, "I'll be back to get them Friday. They want to go to the fair that will be here."

Not wanting to argue I said, "Ok." He walked off and I shut my door. I talked to the kids for a few and then they went in their room to watch TV. Seeing this as a chance to get Monty out of the house, I went to my room. Monty was lying on the bed and watching TV.

"Hey bae," I said. "The kids are in the room. You can tiptoe out."

"Bae, I'll just stay in the room all day. I don't want to leave you. My brother's house is a drag and Shonda is sure to come hassle me. I'm still in pain from the fight with Missy. Let me heal here with you. I'll be quiet in here. I promise."

Never knowing how to say no to him, I nodded my head in agreement. Suddenly, there was another knock on the door. Feeling frustrated and thinking it was Kevin again, I left out of the room to answer the front door. Opening the door, I was surprised to see the detective that was investigating my house fire.

"Hi," I said to him. He'd stopped by when I first moved to ask me more standard questions. Answering all these questions was getting sickening.

"Hello, I'm sorry to just drop by. I called your phone but the answering machine came on," he said.

"It may be dead," I said.

"Well, I just wanted to inform you that we just arrested your ex-husband for the arson on your house."

"What?" I asked. Did Kevin try to kill me? I thought to myself. "Did you find evidence?"

"Well, I can't get into many details but there was something found at the scene that belonged to him. And he doesn't have an alibi. We're charging him with felony arson in the second degree," the detective told me.

My mouth dropped open. Though others suspected him, I never did. Apparently, I was wrong and the police had some sort of evidence. "What was found?"

"Ma'am, we can't divulge many more details. I just wanted you to know because I know the two of you have kids," he told me. "He'll probably sit a couple of weeks then get a bond if he gets a good lawyer. Before he gets out, it'll be wise of you to file a restraining order and file for full temporary custody of the kids with no visitation. The fire could have killed you."

My mouth was still open and my head was spinning. "Ok," I told the officer. "I'll do as you suggested. Thank you for stopping by."

"No problem ma'am," he said. "You have my card if you have any questions. I'll be in touch."

I nodded my head and he walked off. Locking the door, I went to check on the kids. They were watching a cartoon movie. They saw me and I smiled and waved. Then, I headed back to my bedroom to let Monty know what was going on. Kevin was in jail and I'd be raising my kids as a single mom.

CHAPTER 32

TASHA

It had been a week since the funeral. The first few days Tyvonna was sad and wasn't talking much. She wasn't even playing with Teriana as much. Ty took her out for some quality time and they had their private talks. We also let her sleep in the room with us a couple of nights. In these last couple of days, she'd been better. She was back to talking to Teriana and sleeping in her room. We'd also looked into scheduling her some counseling sessions. It had to be hard to lose a mother at such a young age.

My house was feeling big and lonely. Ty had taken a few weeks leave from work. He wanted to be around more for Tyvonna. It hurt him to see her hurt. Today, he decided to put some meat on the grill out back and I decided to invite Mom, Nitra and Sandy over to eat. We all were going through things and I just wanted to be around them all. Mom and Bernard arrived first. This would be the first time that I would be around Bernard since they made up. Realizing mom was grown, I vowed to be nice. As soon as I greeted them, the doorbell rang again. It was Nitra and the kids. I'd told her Monty was invited but she didn't bring him. Bernard went on the back patio to help out Ty. Nitra's kids gave me a hug and went in the den with the other kids. Mom and Nitra followed me into the kitchen.

"You need help preparing anything?" she asked me. "I brought some potato salad. What else are you having?"

"He has ribs, chicken, steak, hot dogs and hamburgers on the grill. I made tossed salad, macaroni and cheese, red beans and rice. Now that we have your potato salad, we're good," I told her.

"That's what's up," Nitra said. "It was good to get the kids out of the house and around their cousins. They're so used to going to their dad on weekends."

"Yea, I know they are," I told her. "I hate that my niece and nephew are going through this. Kevin has really changed. Love can make you do crazy things but arson? He's lost his mind."

Nitra was quiet. "They won't tell me exactly what evidence they have. It's just hard to believe someone that I've been with since a teenager can do this."

Mom shook her head. "It's hard for me to believe it too but the police know what they're doing. Shit, you would think it would be hard for me to believe that my sister sucked my man's dick! We live in a crazy world."

"Yes we do," I said and shook my head. "We have murderers in this world too. Who the hell murdered Latisha? She was a single mom. She didn't deserve to be killed."

Mom just shook her head. "How is Tyvonna holding up? I've been thinking about her a lot lately."

"She's doing better," I said. "It's going to take time though."

"Damn, we're all going through a lot," Nitra said. The doorbell rung again and I looked through the peephole to see that it was Sandy and Lea.

"Hey!" I told them, smiling. Sandy and I had chatted on the phone but we hadn't seen each other in a week or so.

"Hey," she said. Lea ran to where the other kids were and Sandy followed me to the kitchen. She gave Nitra and mom hugs. "How's everyone?"

"As well as can be," I told her.

"That's so sad about Latisha. It just feels so weird. How was the funeral?" Sandy asked me.

"It was sad, especially from Tyvonna's point of view. Missy was there. You know she and Latisha were becoming good friends. After the funeral, we went to eat at her cousin Leslie's house and the bitch Missy got rude with me. I ignored it because of the occasion. Otherwise, I would have slapped her ass." I told them about what happened.

"Wow!" Sandy said. "Just let her slide since her only friend died. She's even more miserable now."

We all sat around and caught up on what was going on with each other. Nitra would soon be awarded full custody of the kids because of Kevin's charges. He hadn't raised the bail money to bond out of jail.

Sandy's phone rang, "Hello?" she answered. "What? When? Ok. Come get me from Tasha's house. I can get my car later." She hung up the phone.

"Is everything ok?" I asked her.

"I'm not sure. That was Lee. He has some things to talk to me about," she said.

"What do you think it's about?" I asked her.

"I'll tell you another time," she said. "He's not far, so I'm going on the porch to wait on him." She waved bye to everyone and walked out of the door. What the hell did her and Lee have going on? I thought to myself.

CHAPTER 33

LEE

The shit that I had to tell Sandy was going to blow her mind! My boys and I had been investigating things because I was going to find out who the big connect was and he was going to pay for having me kidnapped. He was responsible for Sandy being violated. Seeing her being forced to suck someone else's dick hurt my soul. She didn't deserve it. Everything she risked was for me. The experience made me fall in love with her more and see the strong woman that she was. It made me want to give her the world and take back every bad thing that I'd done to her. Because of this, I wouldn't rest until I found the bastard and killed his ass.

My boys and I had found out some shit today. We were close to identifying who the guy was. I pulled into Tasha's driveway and saw Sandy walk off of the porch. Looking at Tasha's big house, I vowed to buy Sandy one just as big or bigger. "Hey bae," she said as she got in the car.

"Hey sexy," I told her as I drove up.

"So, what do you have to talk to me about?" she seemed worried.

"My guys and I found out some important information. We found out the guy that held me in the car was one of the big connect's sons. He has another son who works for the organization too."

"Ok," she said nodding her head. "Do you know their names?"

"I know the name of the guy that assaulted you and held me captive. His name is Derrick or something. We don't know his brother's name yet but we're close. We also may have an address. Everything is planned out and we plan to run up on them tomorrow. It's supposed to be when their daddy meets up with them to collect the big money. Fuck names, we'll have them all in one spot," I told her.

Sandy was quiet. She just stared into space. Finally, she said, "So what's the plan?"

"You don't need to know the plan," I told her. "I just wanted to tell you everything and let you know that things will be handled."

"How are you going to handle things?" she asked. "I don't want you to get hurt baby. It's not worth it."

"You're worth everything baby," I told her. "But, there's no need to worry. Things will be quick and I'll be getting your money back plus more and handle that fucker that violated you." She sat quietly as I pulled into our driveway. We got out of the car and entered our house. Because of our past, I felt the need to tell her the truth about everything.

"You ok baby?" I asked her. "You're mighty quiet."

"I'm ok," she told me. "I love you baby. Please be careful."

"I love you too," I told her. "And don't worry baby, I'm going to be careful." I hugged her tightly. Taking her in the room, I laid her down and made love to her. I was falling in love with Sandy all over again. It bothered me badly all the ways that I mistreated her in the past.

CHAPTER 34

NITRA

Sandy had been in such a hurry to leave with Lee that Tasha told her that Lea could spend the night with her. Tasha, Mom and I continued making the sides for the meat. Things felt normal even though they were far from normal for all of us. Ty came into the kitchen carrying a pan of meat. Bernard came in behind him carrying something also. It was hard to view Bernard the same. He used to seem like a quiet guy who was strong enough to love my mom. Now, he seemed so sneaky. Mom said she was fine and learned some things about him. She felt that their marriage would work. How could I judge? Not only did I cheat on my husband but because of it, he'd burned our house down. It still hurt me to know that he would try to hurt me. I'd hurt him bad.

"Meat's ready! Let's eat!" Mom announced. She placed everything on the counter accordingly. We fixed the kids plate then had them go in the dining room to sit down while we served them their plates and drinks. Tyvonna seemed to be in good spirits around the kids. She needed this. My kids were happy to be with their cousins and not in our apartment. How was I going to tell them their dad was in jail? I planned on waiting a while before telling them.

After the kids were situated, Tasha fixed Ty's plate and Mom fixed Bernard's plate. There was no man's plate for me to fix but that was a good thing. Kevin being in jail broke my heart. I know he tried to hurt me but guilt always set in because I knew that I was wrong for sleeping with Monty. As if he was reading my mind, a text from Monty came through.

"Hey baby. I miss you. Are you still to Tasha's house?" he texted.

"Yes," I texted back.

"Great," he texted. *"I'm around the corner. I'm going to stop by."*

For a few seconds, I wondered why he thought that he could just stop by without asking me first. He told me that he was going to run errands earlier. He'd been spending nights at my apartment but it was only late nights while the kids were asleep. They didn't need to see Mommy lying up with a man right now.

I texted back, "*Ok.*"

Looking up from my phone, Tasha was staring at me. "Monty's going to stop by," I told them. "Is that cool?"

"Yea, it's cool," Tasha said.

Ty said, "Yea its cool sis. I would love to catch up with him." He was always being a nice guy.

About ten minutes later, Monty texted that he was outside. I went to the door to let him in. He spoke to everyone in the kitchen. The kids were still in the dining room.

"Hey man," Ty said. He offered Monty a seat where he was sitting with Bernard. Before sitting, Monty hugged Mom and Tasha. They greeted him with smiles. It made me feel good that they were accepting of him. Tasha had to feel awkward because she was used to him being with Missy for so long.

Things went smooth. We all ate and chatted. Bernard's phone rang then he stepped out of the kitchen to answer it. The expression on Mom's face showed that she wasn't happy about him taking the call in private. She didn't get up from her seat though. Within a few minutes, Bernard came in the kitchen and announced that he had to leave.

"Where are you going?" Mom asked him.

"There's an emergency with my sons. I'll tell you about it when I get home later." Looking at me and Tasha he asked, "Can y'all get y'all Mom home for me?"

"Of course," I spoke up. He kissed Mom and left.

"Mom, you ok?" Tasha asked her.

"Yes," Mom said. "I know about his sons. We're fine. I'm not mad that he left."

I smiled. She didn't seem mad at all. Maybe they were at a happy place. We all chatted for a few. Ty and Monty went out on the deck to talk for a while. After a while, I got a text from Monty asking was I ready to go.

"Yes," I texted back.

"Mom? You about ready to go?" I asked her. "I'm taking you home tonight."

"Yea," she said. She was holding TJ whom had fallen asleep. She went to lay him in the playpen in the den where the kids were.

"Tell the kids to come on," I told her.

As she told them to get ready to leave my daughter asked her, "Grandma, can I stay with you tonight?"

Smiling my mom said, "Sure. You and your brother can stay. Your mom could use a break."

"Thanks mom," I told her. There was no way that I was turning down that offer. Ty and Monty walked into the kitchen. We all said our goodbyes. I dropped Mom and the kids off to her house. Monty met me at my apartment. When I pulled up, he was already parked and standing out of his car in front of my building. Getting out of the car after parking, I walked up to him.

"Hey sexy," he told me.

"Hey bae," I said to him and smiled. Sometimes he seemed too clingy but I really liked him. It felt different being with someone other than Kevin. We were still standing outside when a car pulled up screeching its tires. Irritated by the sound, I looked over at the car. That's when I noticed the driver get out of the car. It was Missy. Walking towards us she said to Monty, "Nigga, you got time to spend with this bitch but don't have time to spend with your kids."

"Man, what the fuck are you doing here? How did your crazy ass know where I was?" he asked her.

"That doesn't matter. What matters is that you're with this bitch and your kids were asking about you," she told him. She was facing us but not up in our face. The space between us was safe space.

Wanting to address the bitch comment, I decided against it. Things needed to be peaceful so my neighbors wouldn't come outside. There were noticeable bruises on her face. It must have been from their fight days ago. It made me wonder just how bad their fight was. Monty's words interrupted my thoughts.

"Missy, how would I know my kids were asking about me?" He was trying to remain calm. "When I tried to talk to you about visitation and getting my kids more, you attacked me. Shonda won't answer her phone for me. How am I supposed to see my kids?"

"Nigga you attacked me! Don't front in front of this bitch," she told him. She looked so crazy. It was actually sad.

"Look. Stop yelling and please don't call her a bitch," Monty told her.

"Oh, so you defending her?" she asked. The hurt could be heard in her voice. I actually felt bad. At one time, she was my sister's good friend. Now, I was standing out here with her man. It had to be hard for her to watch.

"Missy, please leave. We don't want people calling the police. I would love to see my kids. Please tell Shonda to call me. She can pick them up from you and bring them to me tomorrow," the sincerity could be heard in Monty's voice.

"Shonda's your sister. You call her!" Missy said. "And your kids are in the car. You can see them now!" She walked over to the car. Monty and I looked at each other. In the next minute, we saw Lil Monty and his sister get out of the car. "Go hug y'all daddy," Missy told them. Seemingly scared, they slowly walked toward Monty and me. Getting closer, they picked up the pace. They gave their dad a hug when they reached him.

"Hey daddy," they both said. They seemed very happy to see him but reluctant to even look at me. I'm sure their mom had been acting crazy and the fight had to have them on edge.

"Hey babies," Monty said greeting them. "Good to see you. Would you like to spend the day with me tomorrow?" They nodded their heads yes. Before another word could be said, we heard the sound of a car cranking up and pulling off. Looking at the parking lot, we noticed that Missy had sped off. Did this bitch just pull off and leave us with her kids? I thought to myself.

CHAPTER 35

SANDY

After Lee and I made love, I fell asleep. When I woke up to use the bathroom, I noticed that he wasn't in the bed. I checked around the rest of the house and he was nowhere to be found. He'd probably left to get something to eat since I was sleeping. Lee was a late-night owl. Opening the front door, I checked the driveway. His car was gone. I dialed his number on the phone but it went straight to voicemail. Thinking of what we discussed, I sure hoped he wasn't doing anything stupid. Starting to get nervous, I went in my bedroom to check his weed stash. Thankfully, there was some there. Needing to calm down, I rolled a joint of his loud. I relaxed on the bed as I smoked.

Just as I was going to fall asleep again, my cell phone rung. Seeing Lee's phone number flash on the screen, I answered quickly.

"Baby, where are you?" I asked.

"I can't say over the phone," Lee told me. "In a couple of hours, I'm going to call you with a location to come get me."

"What happened? Is everything ok?" I began to worry.

"Just make sure you're up and answer the phone when I call back. I got to go. Love you baby," he told me before hanging up. Now I was more worried than ever. Putting my phone on the charger, I showered and put on some jeans and the first shirt that I pulled out of the drawer. When he called, I planned on being ready.

~

As promised, Lee called later and gave me a location to pick him up from. It was a house on the West side of town, which was shady looking. Men were on the porch when I pulled up. Lee and his cousin walked to my car. Lee got in the passenger side and his cousin got in the back.

"Hey baby," he told me. "I need you to drop Shawn off to his girl's house. It's in route to our house."

"Ok," I told him. Of course, I wanted to know what happened but decided to wait until his cousin was out of the car.

"Good looking out ma," Shawn said and he told me his girlfriend's address.

When I pulled up to the house, Shawn slowly got out of the car.

"Make sure you take care of yourself cuz," Lee told him. "I love you nigga. I'll talk to you tomorrow."

"Love you too man," Shawn said. "It was worth it." It wasn't until he walked on to the porch and into the house that I noticed his arm was wrapped up in bandages.

Once he got in, I pulled off. "What happened to him?" I asked Lee.

"Baby, I can't tell you every detail but he got shot. Luckily, the bullet only hit his arm and didn't do much damage. We were able to get someone to patch it up," he said.

"He got shot? What happened? Did y'all go where I think you went?" I asked him. Shit, he could have at least told me where he was going. What if he'd been hurt?

"Baby, everything's handled. I got your money back plus more cushion for us. The guy who assaulted you was there. We thought he was alone at first. We robbed and shot his ass. After we were in the car about to pull off, some guy came from the backyard shooting and Shawn got hit. It was a flesh wound luckily so he'll be fine," Lee told me.

My head was spinning a mile a minute. Part of me was happy that the fuck nigga who made me suck his dick got shot but part of me was nervous that bad consequences could happen.

"Did the guy you shot die? Did the guy who shot Shawn see your face? These people are dangerous Lee!" My panic set in. I never had a problem fighting and I knew the street life but ever since Lee got into the drug game, my life was beginning to feel like a movie. The movie was getting scary. Where was my normal life as a single mom?

"Baby, calm down and drive us home. Everything's good. We had on masks. It just looks like a normal robbery. I don't know if he's dead but I pray that the bastard is dead. That nigga violated you in front of me. Ain't no way in hell that I could let that shit slide!" Lee said loudly. It felt good that he loved me enough to take that risk but part of me was scared as hell. Lee used to always hang in the streets but he'd never been a killer or robber. All this shit was scaring me. I didn't say much else during the car ride home. He told me not to worry and to forget everything that happened. He made me swear not to tell Tasha any of this. There was no way in hell that I was going to tell her this shit anyway. Finally, we made it home. Once we got in bed, we cuddled and I fell asleep in his arms.

CHAPTER 36

TASHA

The next morning, I fixed the kids breakfast. Ty had gone to buy a trampoline for the backyard so that they can burn some energy. After they ate, they washed and put on clothes. I tidied up the house. TJ was in his swing biting on the teething ring. Ty came back and set up the trampoline and the kids ran outside to jump. Not long later, the doorbell rang and I knew it was Sandy. She'd said that she was on the way to come get Lea.

We hugged and went to sit on the back deck to watch the kids and chat. She seemed nervous about something.

"Are you ok?" I asked her.

"Yea, I'm good. I'm just tired. Lee's been so sweet lately but he's also been keeping me up, if you know what I mean," she smiled. It was obvious that she saw Lee in a different light. He must have really changed and I hoped he kept it up. We sat and talked for about an hour then she said her and Lea had to go. I walked her out to her car. Mom pulled up with Nitra's kids. I'd told her to let them come over and play on the trampoline.

Nitra hadn't called yet but I knew she needed some free time because she was stressed.

"Hey Ms. Karen," Sandy said hugging my mom. "How's everything?"

"Bernard was out all night. He came home late upset. His son got shot," Mom said. She had a worried look on her face.

"Really?" I asked. "Is his son ok?"

"I'm not sure," she said. "The last time we talked he was still in ICU. He's been checking in with me but didn't come home yet. He insists that I don't come to the hospital."

"Dang," I said and Mom and I started walking towards the house with the kids. Sandy said she was sorry about Bernard's son and got in her car. She waved goodbye and pulled off. Nitra's kids ran to the backyard to join the other kids on the trampoline. Mom and I sat on the back porch and watched them. Ty was in the yard talking with them while they jumped. He had TJ in his hands.

I poured us some wine so mom could relax and try not to worry about Bernard. After a couple of hours passed, we fed the kids. Ty went to Popeye's and got a lot of chicken and some sides.

"Call Nitra," Mom told me while we were cleaning the kitchen. "I'm going to bring her kids to her house. I just want to be free in case Bernard needs me later."

"Ok," I said. "I'm surprised she hasn't called you yet to get the kids anyway."

"Cause she's probably laying up with Monty," Mom said disapprovingly. The kids were in the den, out of earshot. "Her life has been hell since she started sleeping with him. She ruined a good marriage."

"It wasn't all that good," I said, trying to defend Nitra. "Kevin dropped the ball on the marriage and his crazy ass tried to kill her."

Mom shook her head and said, "Something tells me that he didn't do it. We've known him for years. He's not capable of doing something like that."

"Well, the police think he's capable," I reminded her. "They don't lock you up without evidence." Mom just shook her head as if she wasn't buying it. Grabbing my phone, I texted

Nitra to let her know the kids were here with Mom and she could pick them up or we could drop them off. Just as I put my phone down, Mom's phone rang. It must have been Nitra.

"Hello?" she answered. "What? Noooo! I'm so sorry baby! I'm coming to you now!" Mom sounded as if she was panicking.

"What's wrong?" I asked her as she hit the end button on her phone.

"Bernard's son died. I've never even met him! I have to go be with Bernard," she said as she grabbed her keys and purse.

"Oh no! Tell him I'm sorry to hear that! Maybe I should go with you?" It seemed only right. He was my stepbrother though I hadn't met him yet.

"Bernard is private," she said. "He didn't even want me at the hospital but I know he needs me now. Once we're home and settled, I'll call you to come around our house. Tomorrow will be good. Tonight's going to be hard for him." Mom looked like she wanted to cry. It was going to be a hard night for her too.

"You're right," I told her. I wanted to be there for her though. "Call me if you need anything. I can even drop you and Bernard off some food. I mean it mom. *Anything.*"

"Ok baby," she told me and hugged me. Walking her to the door, I sighed. First, Tyvonna's mom had been killed. Now, mom's stepson had been shot and killed. And if I thought further, someone was trying to kill Nitra in a house fire. Was our family cursed?

"I love you mom," I told her. "Text me when you make it to the hospital."

"I will baby," she said and got in her car and left. Sadness overwhelmed me as I walked back in the house to fill Ty in on everything.

CHAPTER 37

NITRA

After Missy sped off, Monty and I took the kids inside. It was my first time meeting them so I offered them a snack and something to drink. They accepted the offer though they looked sad. I suggested Monty to take them in my kids' room and talk to them and let them watch TV until they fell asleep. Once he was done, he came in my bedroom. By the look on his face, it was obvious that he was exhausted. He sat on the bed and I got behind him and rubbed his back and shoulders.

"What the fuck is wrong with Missy?" he asked but he couldn't have been expecting an answer. "For her to drop the kids off like that is crazy. And how the hell does she know where you stay?"

Shaking my head, I said, "I don't know bae. I didn't want to disrespect her in front of her kids but she really tried it. We never liked each other so for her to come to my house is crazy. Maybe I should take out a peace warrant on her so that she could stay away."

Monty shook his head. "No, fuck getting police involved. She isn't going to fuck with you. I'll whip her ass if she ever even tried it. I do feel that she and I need to come to a common ground for the kids. She's hurt but she needs to move on. All that drinking and drugging isn't healthy for her."

Thinking of their fight I said, "How could you think you can have a normal talk with her? You're both still healing from the bruises of your last talk or shall I say fight?"

"Well, what should I do? I can't have her dropping the kids off. This is not my home and I'm not sure staying with my brother and I will be good for them," he said sounding frustrated.

"I don't have the answers," I told him. "Let's just get some rest. Maybe she'll come to her senses by tomorrow."

He sighed. After being silent for a few minutes he said, "Roll up that weed that we put up earlier. I need to think."

"Ok bae," I told him then went to do as he told me.

It wasn't long before we were high and laughing at the show on TV. Monty turned to me and said, "I love you woman. There was something special about you ever since we met."

Not knowing what to say, I smiled. Of course, I had love for him but I wasn't sure that I was in love with him. Sometimes I felt that I was. Then there were times that I felt that we were moving too fast. He leaned in and kissed me. There was something about his kiss that made me feel warm and fuzzy.

"You love me girl?" he asked me when we finally came up for air.

"Yes baby," I told him. He had me feeling some type of way. It was a good type of way. He was way more passionate than Kevin was. That's what attracted me to him more. His swag was thuggish but he could be so sensitive and loving.

After I said that, he smiled. The sly smile he gave me let me know what was next. He stripped my clothes off of me then took off his own clothes. He wanted some of this good pussy.

"You're so sexy baby," he told me then kissed my lips again. His kiss got my juices flowing. Sucking my nipples made me even wetter, so I moaned. "Damn that sexy moaning makes me hard." Letting my nipples up for air, he eased his dick into my pussy and stroked me slowly. It wasn't long before he was moaning with me. Slowly, we made love until we came at the same time and he fell asleep with his dick still in my pussy.

~

The next morning, it was back to reality. Monty woke the kids up and fixed them cereal. I had extra toothbrushes that they used. While they ate, Monty and I sat in the living area and talked.

"So, what's the plan?" I asked him. "Are you going to call Missy to get the kids back?"

"No, that bitch needs to get her mind right. I tried calling my sister Shonda when I first woke up but she didn't answer. I sent her a text asking her to call me ASAP. She can help me with Missy because they're close. I'm going to ask her to keep her niece and nephew until I figure things out," he said while glancing at his phone. He must have been hoping Shonda or maybe even Missy called.

"Why don't you just keep them? She's not stable and Shonda seems to be on her side. Your brother is their uncle, so he shouldn't mind them staying there with you," I told him. The Missy that I saw last night was not the Missy that I knew her to be. It was obvious she needed space and time to heal. In my opinion, the kids didn't need to be back with her.

"Maybe," he said. "It depends on Shonda's attitude. Unless you let us stay here with you for a while?"

Immediately, I balled my face up. Was he crazy? "I can't do that bae. My kids won't understand a man and his kids staying here. They're used to Kevin and they're already adjusting to not seeing him. I'm sorry."

"I thought you loved me?" Monty asked. There was a hint of anger in his voice.

"I do," I said. "But my kids are going through so much. My family is going through so much. Now is not the time to move a man and his kids into my small, temporary apartment. I'm getting my life on track too. Missy's crazy ass isn't my only problem."

Looking offended he said, "So moving a man and his kids in is a problem? Missy isn't your problem but she's mine. If you're going to be with me then that makes her your problem too."

"No it doesn't," I told him with attitude. "My mom is going through shit. My sister is dealing with shit. Hell, I'm dealing with the fact that my husband tried to kill us. This is all too much for me right now!" He had to understand that I wasn't trying to be mean but this was all too much. He needed to handle his kids on his own or with his family.

Standing from the couch, he walked into the kitchen. "Kids come on. We're leaving to go see your uncle."

"Ok," they said in unison. They seemed content to be with him but I knew that they were going through so much. I really felt bad for them.

"You're leaving right now baby?" I asked him. Arguing was something that I hated but some things needed to be said. That didn't mean that I wanted them to leave now.

"Yes," he said. "There are some things that I need to figure out." They all walked to the door.

"Ok," I told him. "Call me soon."

"Ok," he said and he and his kids left. He didn't even kiss me or hug me goodbye as he usually did. Feeling bad, I didn't know what to do.

After smoking the weed he left to calm my nerves, I fixed me some food. Finally, I grabbed my phone out of my room. Once I saw Tasha's text message, I texted her that I was on the way to get my kids. Monty forgot that my kids had feelings too and I didn't want to confuse them like he and Missy had done with their kids. Their babies had to be a nervous wreck seeing their brawl. Grabbing my keys and purse, I headed to Tasha's house.

CHAPTER 38

TASHA

Nitra arrived and I fixed her a drink. She looked like she needed it. She was devastated when she found out what had happened to Bernard's son.

"So much is going on," Nitra said. "I feel really sorry for Bernard and his family. Last night Missy brought her ass to my house and dropped off her kids and left. We live in a crazy world."

"What?" I asked her. Missy came to her house? She filled me in on everything that happened with Missy dropping the kids off and with Monty asking to move in.

"Damn sis," I told her. "I agree with you. Monty is tripping. You're going through divorce and your husband is in jail. The kids don't need to deal with a new man and more kids in your house. If he doesn't understand that then fuck him. He can get a place and get his kids. At the end of the day, he was wrong for cheating on Missy with you so she's acting out in hurt. Now he has to deal with the consequences of his actions."

"True," Nitra said. "We both have to deal with them. We both fucked up. I wish that I can put things back how they were and do counseling with Kevin."

"Sis, it is what it is. Kevin and Missy have blame in this too. And no matter what you did, his ass is still wrong for the fire. That shit is still crazy to me. You could have been burned badly or even died in the fire."

"It's true," Nitra said then changed the subject and asked, "Have you talked to mom yet?"

"She texted me saying that she made it to the hospital but that's all that I heard from her," I told her. The kids finally saw that Nitra was there and ran into the kitchen.

"Mommy!" Nitra's daughter said hugging her. Her son hugged her too. My heart ached for my niece and nephew because Kevin had been a good dad and good provider for them. It was heartbreaking knowing they were losing their dad to jail. Looking over at Tyvonna, I remembered the heartbreak that she was dealing with too. Emotions overcame me and I started to feel sad for the kids.

Ty walked in. He came over and kissed me. "You ok bae?" he asked me.

"Yes. Are you?" I asked him.

"Yes," he said. "Let's order the kids some pizza."

"Sounds good to me," I told him.

An hour later, the kids were eating pizza and Nitra and I were sitting in the den and drinking. Out of nowhere, we heard what sounded like glass breaking outside. Curious to see what was going on, Nitra and I ran to the window.

"What the fuck!" we both said at the same time showing we were true sisters. We ran to open the front door. Ty came up behind us. Reaching outside, I noticed that it was Missy. This bitch had a bat in her hand and had busted most of the windows out of Nitra's car.

"Bitch, why the fuck are you in front of my door?" I yelled at her. Ty immediately grabbed me then he pulled out his phone and dialed 911 and told the police what was going on. He used one arm to hold me and Nitra at a distance away from Missy as he called. She just stood there smiling with the bat in her had. This bitch had really lost her mind.

"First, you bring your ass in front of my door and drop off your kids. Now your crazy ass is at my sister's house. I should have beaten your ass a long time ago. Your vibe was always off bitch. There was a reason that I never liked your ass," Nitra said to Missy. By this time, Ty was using both his hands to restrain us from getting at her.

"Missy, you need to leave. The police are on the way and they'll be picking your ass up," Ty said. "Leave now if you don't want to go to jail."

"Fuck you," the bitch Missy told my man. "Tasha's using your dumb ass anyway. You need to make sure that her baby isn't Terry's."

"Bitch, fuck your jealous and miserable ass," I said. Letting the anger take over me, I broke loose from Ty's arms and ran towards her. In my side eye, I saw that Nitra had broken loose too. Reaching Missy, I punched her in the face before she could even react or lift the bat in her hand. I didn't stop punching her as she struggled to fight back. Nitra had come up on her and started hitting her too. Ty tried to break up the mess. In the midst of getting punched, Missy was able to get free from our blows to her face and she swung the bat. Seeing the bat but not able to get out of the way fast enough, I felt the impact on my face and felt dizzy as I fell to the ground.

CHAPTER 39

SANDY

Lee and I were at home talking and chilling. I'd left Tasha's house a few hours ago. It was sad to know that Ms. Karen's stepson had been shot and I told Lee about it.

"Who is her stepson?" he asked.

"I don't know. Neither she nor Tasha have met him," I said. "It's just sad that they're dealing with Bernard's family situation along with Latisha's death. Tyvonna is living with Tasha now and the sad look on that girl's face is heartbreaking. Who would kill her mother?"

Lee sat quiet as if he was in deep thought. Had he heard what I said? Finally he spoke, "Do you think it's a coincidence that Bernard's son got shot last night and so did my cousin. Could his son be the guy we shot who assaulted you?"

Absorbing what he said, I shook my head. "No. I'm sure there were plenty of shootings last night. People get shot all of the time."

"Bernard is secretive," Lee said. "You said even Ms. Karen hasn't met his kids. Maybe it's because he doesn't want her to know about that part of his life. "

"Nah, couldn't be," I said though he had me thinking.

"I'm going to holler at my boys. I'll be back," Lee told me. I was quiet as he hurried out of the house. Was Lee saying that he had shot Bernard's son?

Googling the news, I looked to see if there had been any shootings. The article talked about a guy being shot on the side of a house and being in the hospital with no further details. There was no record of any other shootings last night. That didn't mean anything though. Everyone didn't go to the hospital after being shot. Lee's cousin didn't go after he was shot last night. It was a mighty coincidence though that Bernard's son was in the hospital last night and Lee's crew shot a man last night. I had to figure out if this all was related somehow. Needing to go back to Tasha's house, I dropped Lea off to my mother's. Tasha's mom may even still be there from earlier. Without letting them know what I happened, I had to find a way to figure out who the hell Bernard really was.

CHAPTER 40

NITRA

When I saw my sister get hit with the bat, I lost it. Strength took over me and I snatched the bat out of her hand. Ty was tending to Tasha on the ground. I took the bat and hit Missy with it. I continued to hit her over and over. This bitch had just hit my sister with this same bat and busted my windows just now. She'd left Monty bruised up. The bitch dropped her kids off to my house and just left them. All these thoughts filled my head as I beat this bitch with the bat she came over here with. It was way past time to stick it to this bitch. Everything was a blur until the police pulled me off of her. I didn't realize that they were there.

Realization hit me as I was being handcuffed.

"Sir, she was defending herself and my fiancé," Ty was telling the police when he saw me in handcuffs. Looking over at Tasha, she seemed fine but I saw the bruise on her face. Looking towards Missy, there was a cop helping her. She was still on the ground. Ambulance sirens began to take over. Blood was coming from Missy but it was what the bitch deserved.

"We walked up on an attack," the officer was saying. "She was beating the woman. She could have killed her. We have to take her in."

"Missy came in front of my door and bust out my sister in law's windows. My fiancé and her sister tried to defend themselves. She hit my fiancé with a bat so her sister helped get her off of her. She needs to go to jail. I'm pressing full charges," I'd never seen Ty get angry so it shocked me. I'm sure seeing Tasha get hurt made him angry. "Do you see my fiancé's face?"

"Oh, so she's not the one who hit your wife?" the officer said, referring to me. "I think we assumed that she hit your wife with the bat and beat the other young lady with it too. What exactly is going on here? The other young lady is very seriously injured and in and out of consciousness."

"We came outside and saw her busting my car windows," I said to him, nodding my head towards my car because I was still handcuffed. There was glass everywhere and my windows had big holes. "We told her to leave and he even called you all to stop her. She hit my sister with a bat and I took the bat and hit her in self-defense. She was going to keep hitting my sister and me too. I did what I had to do." Hitting Missy still had me breathing hard. I think that I must have blanked out and lost it on her ass.

The officer looked confused. Was he a damn rookie? "Wait here," he told us and walked over to the other cops who were with Missy. The ambulance had arrived and Missy was in the stretcher. I could see blood coming from her face.

The police officer walked back over and looked at Tasha. "Ma'am, there's another ambulance over there. You can go get checked out."

"I'm fine," Tasha said.

"No baby," Ty told her. "You need to get looked at. They can look at you without taking you to the hospital."

Knowing she was in pain, Tasha nodded in agreement and began to slowly head to the ambulance. Before they walked off good, the officer turned to me. "Ma'am, I have to place you under arrest for assault. We know she instigated it but she's under arrest too for Vandalism to property, assault, and trespassing. She just has to get treated first."

"It makes no sense," I told him. "Look at my sister's face. It was self-defense."

"Ma'am, self defense is a hit or two. You banged her up bad. Hopefully, there's no internal bleeding for her. The way you beat her was more than self-defense. Just get a lawyer and maybe he can help you but I have to arrest you now. If you had hit her a few more times you could have killed that lady."

Tasha looked like she wanted to say something but didn't. Ty spoke, "Sis we're going to come bond you out as soon as I get her checked out and patched up. There's no way these charges can stick. Missy is the only one who needs to be in jail."

"She will be once she's cleared from the hospital," the officer spoke.

"This is some bullshit," I said. The officer just grabbed my already handcuffed arms and led me to the police car. Riding off in the back of the police car, tears fell from my eyes. Why me? Why was I going through so much? What the hell was going on with my life?

CHAPTER 41

TASHA

Seeing Nitra in the police car made me cry. The ambulance lady had just checked me out and bandaged the side of my head. She recommended that I go to the hospital for precaution but I refused. As the ambulance pulled off, Sandy pulled up. The police car had already driven off with Nitra in it. Ty and I were just about to walk in the house.

"What the hell is going on?" Sandy jumped out of the car asking. The last police car and ambulance was just leaving when she drove up. "You ok?"

"Girl, it's a long story. I'm so happy to see you. Come in," I told her. We all walked in the house. Ty went to the den to talk to the kids. I prayed they hadn't been looking out of the window. Sandy and I went to the kitchen.

"What happened to the side of your head?" Sandy asked looking at the gauze the ambulance lady had put on my head.

"Girl, that bitch Missy came round here and busted Nitra's car windows. We went outside to beat her ass and this bitch hit me with the bat. Nitra took the bat and beat her bloody, so they took her to jail. Missy is going to jail AFTER she leaves the hospital. Nitra beat that hoe good. We told the cops it was self-defense and it really was though Nitra went a little far."

Sandy's eyes were wide. "What the hell? I wish I was here when that bitch came around here busting windows. She's really losing it. Nitra needs a lawyer. That bitch hit you with a fucking bat! Damn!"

"Ty is going to get her a good lawyer. I'm just ready for this curse to lift from over my family. Missy will get what she deservers," I sighed.

"Yea I know how you're feeling," Sandy said. It was evident that she was dealing with some things herself but didn't want to divulge. I wasn't going to ask her either because my life was full of enough drama.

Ty walked into the kitchen. He looked upset. "You ok baby?" he came over and kissed me. "You probably should go lie down."

"I'm ok," I said. "I'm more worried about Nitra. Don't you have Monty's number? Can you call and let him know what happened with his psycho baby mama Missy and Nitra?"

"Yea," Ty said and walked out the kitchen door to the patio. He took out his phone to call Monty.

"So, where's your mom? Was she here when all this drama came about?" Sandy asked.

"Thank God she wasn't," I told her. "Sadly, Bernard's son died. She's dealing with her own situation."

Sandy looked shocked. "His son died? Damn! How is he taking it?"

"I don't know," I said. "Mom went to be with him." Sandy just shook her head. I guess she couldn't believe so much was going on. She picked up her phone and started texting. I assumed she was texting Lee. "So, where's Lee and Lea?"

"Lea is at my mom's and Lee is out with friends. I wanted to check on you. Besides, I needed a break from my house," she said. There was something off about her but I couldn't put my finger on what it was.

"Understood," I told her. She didn't have to tell me anything she didn't want to. We fixed a drink and chatted.

CHAPTER 42

SANDY

A realization hit me when Tasha told me that Bernard's son died. If he was who Lee and I thought he was, he would be on the rampage to find out who killed his son. I sent Lee a text telling him what was going on. He told me to keep calm and he would take care of everything. He also confirmed that he had found out that Bernard was in fact the guy that we thought he was.

Tasha and I had a drink and talked. My mind was everywhere, so I couldn't focus. I tried not to act distracted. She'd been calling around trying to get Nitra a bond but they were saying that she had to wait until Monday for her bond hearing. She had to spend two nights in there. That had to be devastating for her. Poor Tasha had to deal with her kids and Tyvonna. Now Nitra's kids would be added to that equation for a few days.

"Damn, what are you going to tell the kids when they ask where their mom is?" I asked Tasha.

"They've already asked and I told them she had to handle something important out of town. They don't mind sleeping over at their auntie's house anyway," she said referring to herself.

"That's true," I said. "Ty can help you get them all off to school. Tyvonna has some kids around to help her get her mind off of things."

"You're right," Tasha said.

~

I'd stayed at Tasha's house a few hours. Lee stopped answering his texts and I got worried. I was sure there was some good reason for why he wasn't answering. There was no way that I was going to sleep until I heard from him though. Thoughts of Bernard kept flashing through my head. Tasha's new step-daddy was a leader of a big-time drug organization and she didn't even know it. Wondering how she would react if she knew, I drifted off to sleep.

CHAPTER 43

LEE

We'd just confirmed who Bernard was when Sandy texted me telling me that his son had died. I was glad the bastard was dead for fucking with me and my woman. They weren't going to just let his death go because of who he was. They were going to search until they found out who did it and why. Because of this, my boys and I came up with a plan to get rid of Bernard and his other son. The plan had to go off without a hitch.

Knowing that Bernard was the leader and that he was married to Tasha's mom gave me a big advantage. Tasha's mom stayed in Tasha's old place so I knew where he laid his head. I just needed to catch him with his other son. I knew of a way to make that happen. It was sunrise when I went home to find Sandy sound asleep. I cuddled on the bed next to her. Sandy and I had been through so much. After all of this was over, I needed to take my baby on vacation.

CHAPTER 44

NITRA

Standing in front of a judge and being dressed in an orange jumpsuit made me cringe. Ty had gotten me a great lawyer and I had been granted a bond. The lawyer also told me that it was self-defense in his eyes and he would get my charges dismissed in court. That made me feel better but it still didn't change the fact that I'd spent two nights in jail.

Finally, they called my name to be released and I put on my original clothes and practically ran out of the place. Expecting to see Tasha waiting for me in the lobby, I was surprised when I noticed that it was Monty. I hadn't called him while I was in jail. It was evident that he and I needed space. Last time I saw him, he'd left my place mad with his kids in tow.

"Hey bae," he said and gave me a hug. I hugged him back and we walked out of the place quietly until we got inside of his car.

"Thank you for coming," I told him.

"Baby, you know that's not a problem. I'm so sorry about getting upset with you. You were right. I was just being selfish. It is too early for the kids and me to move in with you," he told me.

"And that's all that I was saying," I told him. "My kids are going through a lot too."

"I know baby. Shonda and I had a heart to heart talk and she agrees that Missy is unstable. Of course, she blames me for it. She's going to keep the kids at her house during the week to make sure they get off to school and everything. They'll be at my brother's house with me on the weekends and some days after school. I've started searching for my own place so they can be with me all the time," he told me.

Hearing this from him made me feel proud. "That's great baby," I told him. "You're doing the right thing. Missy's ass is going to do some time anyway because we're pressing charges to the fullest. Tasha didn't deserve to get hurt in this and have that bitch come to her house. She's dealing with enough."

"Missy doing time isn't going to help her get better. Besides, you over did the beating on her babe. She's still in the hospital. She has a concussion and so many stitches in different places."

"Oh, so you're taking up for her and you went to see her?" I questioned him. He was annoying me.

"I'm not taking up for her. She was dead wrong. But, she is fucked up bae. You could have killed her. She is my kids' mom, so of course I had to check on her," he told me.

"Whatever," I told him. "That bitch needs serious help. How the fuck did she know where I live? And her showing up to Tasha's house is looney. She went too far and deserves everything that she gets." Monty remained quiet as I talked. I didn't like that he didn't respond.

"Drop me to Tasha's house so I can get my kids. My car is fucked up thanks to your crazy baby mama," I angrily told him. How dare he feel any sympathy for her ass?

"Tasha told me to let you go home and get yourself together. She is picking the kids up from school and feeding them dinner. Then, you can get them or she'll bring them to you if you prefer," he told me.

"How is Tasha? Did you see whether that bitch bruised her up bad?" I asked him.

He sighed then said, "I haven't seen Tasha. We talked on the phone earlier and other than that I've been talking to Ty. I apologized to him for everything and he says Tasha is fine."

We pulled up to my place. I didn't like the vibe between us right now. "Well, thank you for the ride home," I said while getting out of his car. "I'll talk to you later."

"Bae, I was thinking that I could come in and talk to you. Don't act like that."

"Not now. I need to take a real bath and to change clothes. Then, I need to go check on my sister and my mom. My mom is going to be burying her stepson in a few days."

"Ok, I understand," he told me, though I knew he didn't. Once I got into my house, I cried. It was long overdue. I'd actually spent nights in jail. There was all of this drama because of an affair that never should have happened. I prayed to God that things would get better for my family and I.

CHAPTER 45

TASHA

It was the day of Bernard's son's funeral. Wanting to support him and my mom, I insisted on going. Bernard had planned a very private and very small funeral. He acted as if it was some top-secret mission. Everyone mourned differently so Mom helped him plan the funeral that he wanted. Ty stayed home with the kids. Nitra wanted to come support but wasn't up for it so she stayed home too. Sandy insisted on accompanying me so that I won't feel out of place. After persuasion, Bernard allowed her to come. For some reason, he was very strict with the guest list. The fact that he was being cautious was a good thing because his son had been murdered and they had no clue whom had killed him.

Mom rode in the funeral car with Bernard and I drove behind them separately. Sandy rode with me. There were less than 30 people in attendance and they all were family for the most part. Bernard's other son was so upset that he refused to attend the funeral. He didn't want to see his brother get buried 6 feet deep into the ground. Bernard's ex wife, his sons' mother, had passed away years ago. We met Bernard's sister, aunt, uncles, cousins and more family.

The funeral service was sad and had me in my feelings. It just made me think about how short life was and how anything could happen at any minute. We pulled up to Mom's house. There were only a few close family members coming to the house after the service. Others had been given to-go plates at the church. Parking, I noticed Sandy was texting someone.

"What are you and Lee texting about?" I asked her. She'd been texting during the funeral too.

"Nothing," she said looking up from her phone. Seemingly changing the subject, she looked at me and said, "Your bruise has healed."

"It's just about healed but I had to apply extra makeup to make sure it is hidden. That bitch is going to pay for hitting me with that bat. It's sad because she was once our friend," I said referring to Missy.

"Yea it is sad," Sandy said. "But actions have consequences, so that's why her ass is sitting in jail. Something is truly wrong with her."

"She actually just went to jail yesterday. It took a while for her to get out of the hospital."

"Damn," Sandy said. "Nitra must have fucked her up bad."

"Yea, Nitra beat the shit out of her. Once she saw that Missy hit me, she lost it! She doesn't play about her sis," I said smiling. "Hopefully, the lawyer can get her charges dropped. She's going through enough with the fire and Kevin being in jail. He's been calling her but she hasn't accepted his calls."

"I wouldn't either," Sandy said and we got out of the car so that we could go into mom's house.

There were only about 10 or so people in the house. Bernard's other son had yet to arrive. He'd promise to come over after the funeral. We ate some food that Mom had already cooked and had waiting on us. We chatted with Bernard's family who seemed very nice. They must have had some kind of money because they all had nice cars and it was easy to see that the funeral cost a pretty penny. The coffin and everything looked expensive. Bernard must have had money saved or maybe his family helped out.

A couple of hours had passed. We'd been mingling and talking with Bernard's family. Sandy and I were sitting in the den when mama came in. "Tasha, come meet Bernard's son," she said. Sighing, I got up from the chair. Looking at Sandy, I signaled for her to get her ass up with me.

We walked into the kitchen where Bernard was. My eyes opened in shock when Bernard said, "Tasha, meet my son Darrin." My mouth dropped open. Seeing Darrin standing next to Bernard was appalling. Darrin was Bernard's son! I just couldn't believe it!

CHAPTER 46

SANDY

I couldn't move when I recognized Darrin. What the fuck was he doing here? He was Bernard's son? How the fuck didn't we know that? He was never around when I came around Bernard. Tasha's mouth was open so she was just as surprised as I was. So many questions came through my head.

Bernard was talking but I couldn't even understand what he was saying. I locked eyes with Darrin. This was the first time I'd seen him since he left me broken and hurt. Bernard was his dad? As teens, his dad had never been around. Maybe when he moved to another city years ago they reconnected. The look he gave me let me know that it was a surprise to him too.

Tasha finally spoke, "Darrin? You're my new stepbrother? How come we had no clue?" she asked.

"My family is secretive," Darrin said. He looked over at me. "Good to see you Sandy. You look really good."

I just looked at him. So many thoughts went through my head. So, it was Darrin's brother who assaulted me? Did he know? He had to have known that Lee was kidnapped. Did he know it was Lee? He had to have been there when Lee and his cousins ran in their spot. Lee hadn't seen his face because he came out of the back shooting at the last minute. Damn! Darrin was the one who shot Lee's cousin!

"Are you ok?" Tasha asked me. She had no clue the thoughts that were in my head and what was going to happen later. Lee and his team had planned to take revenge tonight! Should I call and tell Lee to call off his plan? Tasha led me out of the room and back into the den.

"Sandy, are you ok?" she asked me again once we were alone.

"Yes," I finally said. "It's just shocking to see Darrin! Bernard is his dad? Wow!"

"Right! I'm shocked too," Tasha said. At that moment, Darrin walked in and invaded our privacy.

"Sandy, we need to talk. My emotions are all over the place right now because my brother is dead. He was my best friend in the world. Still, I feel there are some things that I need to talk to you about," he said.

"I'm so sorry about your brother Darrin. We've known each other since high school but I didn't even know you had a brother. And I've met Bernard several times and didn't even know he was your dad. It's like you had a secret life. What we had wasn't real," I told him. Old feelings were coming back and I didn't know what to do. Guilt started overwhelming me. Feelings of hurt came over me. My emotions were a mess.

"I know and I'm sorry," Darrin told me. Then he looked at Tasha and said, "Tasha can I have just 5 minutes alone with Sandy?"

"Ok, new stepbrother," Tasha said as she left the den. I knew that she was just trying to lighten the mood. It was so much to take in.

Darrin sat next to me. It made me feel weird. The feelings that I had for him ran deep and it made me realize that. I had to focus and remember what his brother did to me.

"Sandy, I'm sorry that you didn't know about my dad or brother. There are certain things in the family business that we don't divulge and I'm truly sorry. I loved you with all my heart. Seeing you in the video having sex with Lee let me know that you still had feelings for him and it crushed me. That's why I decided to walk away from our relationship," he told me sounding sincere.

Knowing that he was right about my feelings for Lee, I couldn't argue with that. My feelings for him were still real too. It still hit me that he may have known about Lee getting kidnapped but I couldn't let on that I knew what type of business he was really in. Things were feeling so crazy. "I understand," I told him. I started to question the plan that Lee had. It was a whole other ball game now that I knew Darrin was Bernard's son. The plan already had me feeling uneasy because I would be betraying Tasha. It had to be done though or Lee wouldn't be safe. They would eventually find out who killed Bernard's son, then they would surely kill Lee and his family. What the hell should I do? It didn't seem that I had any other choice except to follow through with the plan. Promises were made to me that Tasha and her mom wouldn't get hurt in the plan. That was the only reason that I went along with it.

"Can we call a truce?" Darrin was saying. My thoughts had drowned him out for a minute or so. "We both handled

221

things wrong. Let's forget the past and be friends. We've known each other a long time. Friends are important and I really need a friend now. My brother is dead bae. I'm also in shock that Tasha's my new stepsister. I truly wish my brother would have had a chance to meet you all." Darrin sounded sad. My heart was beating fast.

"Yes. We can call a truce," I told him. Feeling knots in my stomach, I got up. "I have to use the restroom. Good seeing you."

"Ok cool," he told me. "Good seeing you too. I wish it was under better circumstances." He got up and went back in the kitchen with the others while I made my way to the restroom. I dialed Lee's number on my cell phone. He didn't pick it up. I dialed it again. There was still no answer. Figuring he wasn't going to answer right now, I decided to call things off. Lee and I needed to talk about some things first.

"We have to call it off. I'll tell you why later." I texted Lee hoping that he would get it in time.

After actually using the bathroom, I washed my hands and went back to where the guests were. Tasha was standing in the kitchen talking to her mom. I walked up to them.

"Hey. Everything good?" Tasha asked me. I knew she was referring to my conversation with Darrin.

"Yes, Darrin and I decided to be cool," I told her. My thoughts were on Lee and wondering what the hell he was doing. I prayed that he got my text message in time.

"Well that's good. I wish it weren't under these sad conditions," Tasha said. "It's obvious he still has feelings for you."

"Where are the guys?" I asked looking around the house. Choosing to ignore her was my best option.

"Bernard and Darrin went to walk some of their family out to the car," Tasha told me. Ms. Karen started covering up the food. Everyone had eaten well. Tasha's mom had prepared most of the food. There were some dishes prepared by Bernard's family. They didn't trust to eat the food that was prepared by people giving the family condolences.

"Oh," was all I could say. My mind was occupied with all kinds of thoughts. Were Lee and his crew down the street as planned waiting for Bernard to come outside? They were going to shoot any man around Bernard but they promised to stay away from women. They knew that me, Tasha and Tasha's mom would be around and didn't want to take any chances. My stomach did flips. I couldn't keep still so I began to help them cover up and put up the food. It seemed awfully silent to me. My nerves were bad. I prayed Lee listened to my text and waited until I could explain things to him.

"What a day," Tasha sighed. "It was sad yet full of surprises." Her mom was quiet as she continued cleaning up the kitchen.

"You got that right," I told her. "It was definitely full of surprises!" My heart was beating a mile a minute. Without warning, we heard what sounded like firecrackers popping off outside. Tasha looked at her mom and me; she had a quizzical look on her face. Knowing it must have been gunshots, I passed out on the kitchen floor.

CHAPTER 47

LEE

We'd been waiting for hours. Earlier, we had parked down the street from Bernard and Tasha's mother's house. They were at the funeral when we gathered in the tinted Ford Expedition and staked out the area. Bernard had power. With his son dead, he was going to do everything possible to find the killers. It was a must that he died first. Our safety was at stake. I, along with five of my goons, sat and waited patiently. Thanks to Sandy, we knew that only a few close family members would be coming to the house afterwards.

The plan was to wait until the guests left and roll up on all of them and kill them. We were only to leave the women alive. We knew that Bernard was going to walk his guests out and we could get rid of him. His other son was bound to be out there somewhere too, so he would also be eliminated. Once they were dead, we would have no more worries and wouldn't have to watch our backs. Sandy's job was to make sure the ladies stayed in the house, if possible. It was possible that Tasha's mom would come outside with her husband and we would make sure she didn't get caught in the crossfire.

After several hours, people could be seen walking out of the house towards their cars. It was do or die. Von, the one who was driving the SUV that we were in, slowly rode up to the house. Before he could stop the car all the way, we all jumped out of the SUV and started shooting. They didn't want to shoot while still inside the van because it would be easy to miss the targets. As soon as we jumped out, we fired our guns. The plan was to catch them off guard so they wouldn't have time to pull their guns.

I saw two of the men hit the ground. The others were running and trying to find cover. There was some women who ran and hid behind a car. At least one of them was able to pull their weapon because a bullet flew right by me and hit one of my men in the shoulders. He ran back inside of the SUV while we continued to shoot it out. The sound of moaning could be heard and I knew that it was one of the men we'd shot earlier. Holding two guns in my hand, I continued shooting while slowly backing up towards the SUV. Seeing people spread out on the ground, I dived back in the SUV with the others. Pain came from the left side of my stomach. It took me a moment to realize I'd been shot. The last thing I remembered was Von pulling off. I heard someone say, "Lee was shot too!" After that, everything faded to black.

CHAPTER 48

TASHA

I didn't know what the hell was going on! We'd heard what sounded like gunshots and Sandy fainted and fell down to the floor. Getting on the floor to see if she was ok, I shook her. She slowly opened her eyes.

"Are you ok?" I asked her.

"Were those gunshots?" I heard my mother ask. "I'm calling the police."

After letting me help her up, Sandy said that she was ok. "What the hell is going on outside?" she asked.

"I don't know. Those were a lot of fucking shots," I cried. Mom told the police what was going on and hung up.

Hearing the front door open scared us. We didn't know if someone was coming in to shoot us. Darrin walked into the house and I felt relief until he said, "Call the ambulance! Dad's been shot but he's still breathing! I gotta go!" Darrin ran back out of the door.

"Bernard! No!" Mom said and she ran outside. Darrin was driving off when I ran out there behind my mom. She'd run over to where Bernard was laying on the ground. It looked as if he'd been shot in the upper chest area or shoulder. Blood was everywhere so it was hard to tell. I saw two people with Darrin in the car driving off. It looked like one of his cousins and his aunt.

I could hear Sandy come out behind me. "I called the police again, so they'd know someone had been shot," she said. As she walked further in the yard, she screamed. Running to her, I saw two dead bodies. One belonged to Bernard's brother and the other belonged to one of his cousins. Seeing the bodies made me throw up. Sandy grabbed me and took me to the porch. Mom was still on the side of Bernard. She was crying and telling him to hold on. Relief came over me as I heard the sirens of the police and ambulance pull up to Mom's house.

CHAPTER 49

NITRA

I'd spent the day relaxing around the house. I hadn't spoken with Monty in a couple of days though he'd been calling. I just couldn't believe all that happened. The kids and I had eaten pizza and watched a movie earlier. They were fast asleep now. They didn't have a clue that their mom had been in jail. Sadly, their dad was still in jail. I was upset at what he did. Was he really trying to kill me? But, I also felt guilty because it was my fault for cheating with Monty.

Monty had been begging to talk with me, so I finally agreed to let him come over tonight. He was on his way. I'd taken a shower and but on a simple cotton dress pajamas. Part of me liked Monty being around. The sex was great and it felt good being held by him. Another part of me knew that I needed some me time to get myself together and fully heal. I needed to get a divorce and worry about the progress of my house being fixed from the fire. My children needed time to adjust being without their father. There was no room in my life for a man right now.

Monty sent me a text message telling me to open the front door. Once inside, he followed me into my bedroom.

"I missed you baby," he told me as he took a seat on the bed.

"I missed you too," I told him.

"You don't act like it," he said.

"It's just too much going on in my life right now. We're getting too caught up. We have to resolve our past issues. Kevin's in jail. The kids are feeling his loss. Now Missy's crazy ass is in jail."

"You're right," he said. "But I don't want to stop seeing you. We can just cut back and take it slow."

"We can do it like that," I told him. We started kissing. His lips felt so warm. We were definitely attracted to each other. The sound of my phone ringing made us break free from our passionate kiss. Seeing Tasha's number come across the phone, I answered.

"Nitra! Bernard's been shot! It's so much going on! Drop the kids to my house with Ty then come to Grady's

Hospital. Mom needs you here! Bernard's in surgery!" she screamed into the phone.

"What!" I was shocked. Bernard had been shot? Tasha just hung up the phone.

"What's happening?" Monty asked me.

"Bernard's been shot. It's the night of the man's son's funeral! This shit is just crazy. She wants me to drop my kids to Ty but I don't want to wake them up."

"I'll stay here with them," he said. Before I could object, he stated "They won't know I'm here. I'll stay in the room until you come back. I'll just be here in case of an emergency."

Needing to see what was going on, I gave in. "Ok. I'll be back really soon. I just need to see what happened. Call me if they wake up." I ran out of the door to the hospital.

~

Entering the hospital, I rode the elevator to the third floor as Tasha instructed. When I reached the floor, I immediately saw Tasha and mom sitting in the waiting room. Running over to mom, I gave her a hug. Looking just as shook as mom, I hugged Tasha. They filled me in on what had happened and I was mortified. Two of Bernard's family members had been murdered and he had been shot. Darrin and other family had all left the house. It was evident that they were going after the shooters. What the hell was going on? What if the bullets had hit my mom or my sister?

"Mom, it isn't safe to stay in your house right now," I told her. "You and Tasha could have been shot!"

"She's going to stay with me," Tasha spoke. "I don't know what the hell is going on. Sandy went home mortified."

"Girls," Mom spoke up. "I need to talk to you about some things." Just as soon as she said that, the nurse came out.

"How is he?" Mom asked her.

"The surgery was successful. We were able to take the bullet out of his stomach and stop the bleeding. It's going to take time to heal but we think he's going to make a full recovery."

"Thank God," Mom said. "Can I see him?"

"Yes," the nurse said, "but just for a few minutes. He has to rest."

Mom went in to see Bernard while Tasha and I waited. Afterwards, Tasha took mom home with her and I went back to my house with Monty and my kids.

CHAPTER 50

SANDY

I went home after leaving Ms. Karen's house. Darrin running in the door had been a shock. They'd missed him as a target. Part of me was happy he didn't get killed and I felt bad about everything with Bernard. He was Ms. Karen's husband but Lee's safety was top priority. Bernard may live, so everything was all for nothing. Two of Bernard's family members, who were a part of his drug army, had been killed. That weakened them but I knew that would make Darrin want to find who did it even more. I prayed that Lee had covered his tracks.

Lee hadn't answered any of my calls and I began to worry. After several hours of me worrying, my phone rang.

"Hello?" I answered sounding frantic.

"Sandy, this is Gunnar. I'm one of Lee's men."

"Where's Lee?" I asked him.

"He's here with me. He's been shot. I'm going to give you an address where we are." My heart sunk when I heard that

Lee had been shot. I got in my car and drove off to the address that Gunnar had given me. It was dark so I quickly knocked on the door of the house. Someone let me in.

"Where's Lee?" I asked. I was led to a room where Lee was hooked up to an IV. There was some lady bandaging him up. "Are you ok? You need to go to a hospital," I told him then kissed his cheek. He looked like he was in pain.

"I'll be fine," he said, moaning. "Can we have some privacy?" he asked the lady and his cousin who was in the room. He wanted to talk to me alone.

"Baby, I tried to get you to call it off. You didn't see my text? I found out that Darrin is Bernard's other son!" I told Lee.

"Darrin? Damn! Who would have thought?" Lee said. "Is he dead? Is Bernard dead?"

Shaking my head, I said, "No. Darrin didn't get hit. He must have been shooting back and hit you. Bernard's in the hospital. There were two men dead though."

"Damn," Lee said. "Well, we'll just lay low. They have no way of finding out who did it. This shit is fucked up. Darrin's fuck ass is Bernard's son! I wish I would have shot his ass right in the head!"

"It'll be ok baby," I told him. "Like you said, just lay low. There is no way for them to really find out who was responsible for the robbery or this shooting. Tell that lady to hurry up and finish patching you up so I can take you home. Let's just let everything go and forget this happened."

CHAPTER 51

TASHA

The next morning after the shooting, Mom went back out to the hospital to be with her husband. Ty had fixed the kids breakfast. I slept in an extra few minutes. Everything that was happening around me had me exhausted. It made me wonder what today was going to bring!

"Hey baby," I told Ty when I walked into the kitchen. TJ was in his hand and he reached for me. I grabbed and kissed my baby. Today, I didn't want to do anything but stay home with my kids. Seeing those dead bodies had me shook. The doorbell rang and I sucked my teeth. Who could this be? Peeping through the peep hole, I saw that it was the police. I thought I'd answered all their questions last night. Mom, Sandy and I didn't see what happened because we were in the house. Police showing up to my house was beginning to become a trend.

"Hi, can I help you?" I asked the officers when I opened the door. Ty was behind me. It was the same officer who came around with Latisha's cousin to tell us she had been killed. What the hell did he want now?

"Yes, I need to speak with Mr. Tyvon Jenkins. It's regarding Latisha Anderson," the officer said. We stepped onto the porch. TJ was still in my hand so I sat down and sat him in my lap.

"Sir, I don't know anything about what happened to her," Ty started saying. We knew her dumb ass cousin was trying to accuse him.

"We know," he told us. Relief came over me when he said that. He continued, "We know who did it."

"Who?" Ty and I both asked.

"We can't give any details at this time. Her cousin is her closet family member, so give her a call and she can tell you," he said. "I just wanted to inform you that we know what happened and our investigation into you is over. We wish you and your daughter the best and sorry about the tragic loss of her mother." Ty nodded his head and the officer left. Sadness came in Ty's eyes when the officer mentioned his daughter. Who the hell killed Latisha?

CHAPTER 52

NITRA

The next day, I got a call from the detective working my house arson case. He asked if he could come over and speak with me about some findings. I agreed. Monty had left earlier that morning. When the detective came, I sent the kids to watch TV in their room.

"How are you?" the detective asked me.

"I'm doing ok. It's still hard to believe that Kevin was responsible for the arson," I sighed.

"Well, that's why I'm here," the detective said. "He wasn't responsible."

"He wasn't?" I asked. I was happy but confused. "Do you know who was? Is he getting out of jail?"

"Yes, he'll be getting out of jail. The process has been started and he should be free in a few hours."

I felt relieved. "I'm really happy it wasn't him. Now my kids could have their daddy back. But who could have set the fire? Was it accidental after all?"

"The person who did it was Missy Rogers," he continued.

"Missy?" I asked him. Thinking I said, "It makes sense. Her ass has been acting really crazy lately. She was arrested recently for vandalizing my car and assaulting my sister."

"I know," he said then he put his head down as if he had more to say. "Missy hung herself in jail last night."

"What?" I asked him. Her ass was crazy but I didn't think she would kill herself!

"There's more. She left a note. In the note, she said she couldn't live without Monty. She also confessed to setting your house on fire because he was in there with you."

"Wow!" my mouth was hanging open. Missy had killed herself! And, she was the one who set the fire! I wasn't prepared to hear all of this. "I have to call and tell Monty!"

"Another officer is telling him now," the detective told me. "I need to tell you the rest. She also confessed to killing her good friend Latisha. Latisha knew about the fire and she said she didn't trust her not to tell."

My mouth opened but I couldn't speak. The detective kept talking but I couldn't hear him. Finally, he left and I nodded and waved goodbye. After the detective left, I sat on my couch not moving. This was all too much! Finally, I got myself together and told the kids to put on their shoes so that we could go to Tasha's house.

Arriving to Tasha's house, she gave me a hug. She hugged the kids as well. My sister seemed really happy to see me.

"Hey," I told her. "Kids go play with your cousins. I have to talk to Auntie Tasha and Uncle Ty in private."

"Everything ok?" she asked me. "A detective came here and told us they found out who killed Latisha so the investigation into Ty is over. He didn't say who didn't though."

"It was Missy!" I blurted out. I told them everything the detective had told me. "So, Kevin is innocent after all! Thank God!"

"Yes, thank God," Tasha said. "I shouldn't have believed he would do such a thing but he definitely had motive."

"He did and he had been acting like an asshole," I told her.

We all were shaken that Missy had set the fire and killed Latisha to cover it up. She had really lost her mind! What could make a woman go so crazy?

~

Later that evening, I called Monty to check on him. He was distressed about Missy killing herself. Though she'd murdered her friend and tried to kill us, he kept saying he couldn't believe it. He didn't know how to tell the kids their mom was dead. His sister took the phone from him and let me know that he needed time to deal with things. I completely understood even though I didn't like her attitude. Kevin had called once he'd gotten out of jail. I apologized to him for everything and he said he was happy to be free and just wanted to see his kids. I let him come take the kids to his house. I sat home alone just thinking about everything that had happened. Life was crazy right now!

CHAPTER 53

TASHA

A few days had passed since we found out that Missy killed herself. I kind of felt bad because at one point she had been my friend. She went crazy over losing Monty and tried to kill him and my sister. She actually succeeded in killing Latisha and now Tyvonna didn't have her mom. My heart ached for that little girl and I vowed to treat her as if she were my own child.

Now that we knew what happened, we could all begin the healing process. Bernard was still in the hospital but he was getting stronger. Mom still stayed with me when she didn't sleep at the hospital. I wished they would find out who had shot Bernard. Mom had told Nitra and I that Bernard was involved in the drug world and she only found out after that incident with Aunt Karen. She said he was getting out of the game but his son's murder and his shooting were probably related. We were scared for mom but she assured us that she would be ok. I hadn't seen Darrin since the funeral but mom said he visited the hospital to see his dad. It was crazy that Darrin and Bernard were father and son drug kings. Darrin had always been more of the nerd type in high school. Mom planned on taking Bernard out of the country to lay low and heal for a while when he left the hospital.

Sandy hadn't answered her phone for me in days. I guess she was laid up with Lee but it wasn't like her to not answer for so long. I needed to tell her all the new developments that were happening, so I decided to go to her place. Ty watched the kids as I drove to Sandy's place. Her car was parked outside and I saw another car. That must have been Lee's car. I had no clue what he was driving these days.

Ringing the doorbell, no one answered. They could have been fucking or something but I wasn't leaving. They'd been lying up under each other enough, so I was interrupting their fun. I began knocking loud so that they could hear me. They still didn't answer.

"Sandy!" I yelled. "Open the door!" After yelling and knocking for a few minutes, there was still no answer. Feeling defeated, I decided to leave and come back later. Before leaving,

I saw a car pull up. Getting closer, I saw that it was Sandy's mom. She had Lea in the car.

"No one's answering," I told her. "I've been knocking and ringing the doorbell for a long time."

"She hasn't answered the phone for me either in a couple of days and I've had Lea this whole time. I know she needed space but I can't take Lea to school tomorrow. I have an appointment. She has to get her child." Lea was still sitting in the car. The windows were down. It felt good outside.

Worry set in my stomach. "It's not like her not to answer for you, if you have Lea. Should we be worried?"

"I'm not sure," her mom said. "I have a key so I'll just let myself in since they didn't answer the doorbell or knocking." She searched her key chain for the right key then walked to the front door. She knocked and rung the doorbell one last time before letting herself in. I stayed on the porch so that I could keep an eye on Lea in the car. Within seconds of her being in the house, I heard her let out a loud, bloodcurdling scream. Running in the house, I didn't see anyone in the living room, so I ran to Sandy's bedroom. My eyes had to be playing tricks on me! I almost passed out when I saw Lee and Sandy laying on the bed naked and bleeding. Lee was dead with a gunshot to the head. Blood was coming from Sandy's stomach area. Her mom called the police and ambulance. She was hysterical. By instinct, I ran over to Sandy crying. I checked to see if she was breathing. It seemed like she was breathing very slightly.

"She's breathing!" I cried to Sandy's mom. "Tell them to please hurry up!" I sat by my friend and cried until the ambulance and police arrived. Sandy's mom left out to wait outside with Lea. Who the hell would shoot them and leave them like this? So many deaths and shootings were around me lately. What the fuck was going on?

EPILOGUE

TASHA

It had been weeks since Lee had been killed and Sandy was been shot. Sandy had been in a coma for days but she finally came out of it. Her gunshot wound messed up her kidneys but she would live. It had been almost a whole day since they'd been shot so Sandy was very blessed to be living. She had a long recovery ahead. When she found out that Lee had died, she lost control and they had to sedate her. It seemed that she was going to lose her mind. Her mom and I were by her side the whole time. We took turns with taking care of Lea. The police were investigating but so far there were no leads on who murdered Lee and shot Sandy. It could have been a robbery gone badly. No fingerprints were found at their house. Sandy kept mentioning Darrin's name for some reason. She had trouble finishing her sentence when she said his name. Maybe she was just remembering that she'd seen him recently. Knowing that she still had feelings for him, I wondered if she just wanted him to be there by her side.

Bernard was recovering good and he and my mom moved to another state. He now walked with a cane but other than that he would be fine. Mom wanted a fresh start with Bernard in a new place. He had pledged to her that he was out of the drug game. I was going to miss her like hell. I had gotten used to her helping out with the kids. She could fly in sometimes to see us. Bernard was sure to have a lot of money that he'd made over the years. Darrin was probably somewhere across the country too or maybe even out of the country. I hadn't seen him since his brother's funeral. I'm sure Bernard knew where his son was.

Nitra was relieved that Kevin was out of jail and wasn't responsible for the fire. Now her kids didn't have to live without their dad. They had a long talk when he got out and decided to become friends so that they could co-parent effectively. Nitra apologized for everything and Kevin accepted it. He apologized to her for being an asshole. Nitra also decided to stop seeing Monty. He had a lot to deal with now that Missy was dead. She'd stopped by to see him a few days ago and give her condolences. His kids needed their dad's full attention to help them heal. Nitra felt she needed to be by herself until after her divorce was official and final. Monty seemed so devastated over Missy. He needed time to heal himself. Nitra seemed to be the last person on his mind these days. Nitra prayed that he didn't blame himself for anything that Missy did.

Ty and I eloped! We decided to take the kids on a vacation for a few days. During that vacation, we decided to elope. Our kids were the only family in attendance at the small wedding chapel. The day was perfect. Ty made vows to my kids and I made a vow to Tyvonna. We all became a family in front of God. It wasn't about a big wedding for everyone to see. It was about being in love and having our kids there. Through everything that had happened to turn our lives upside down, Ty stood by my side and I stood by his. We'd proved that our love could overcome anything. I was finally Mrs. Tyvon Jenkins. I was no longer a single mom. Ty was my king and I was his queen. We would love each other forever.

Sultana Sams is a native of Savannah, GA. She is the mother of three kids, a son and two daughters, whom motivate her and support her love of writing. She holds degrees in Accounting and Business Management. Sultana runs her own personal Bookkeeping and Tax preparation business. Although she loves accounting work, her first love is reading and writing. She published her first book, *"Love, Sex and the Single Mom"* in 2015 but changed the cover and republished it in 2016. It received great reviews so she decided to turn it into a series. Her other published books include *Love, Sex and the Single Mom part 2* and *Driving Me Crazy* and they received 5 star reviews as well.

Made in the USA
Columbia, SC
16 July 2023

20560250R00139